Out to Sea

Festival of Hues

By
R.W.K. Clark

This is a work of fiction. All names, characters, locales, and incidents are
the product of the author's imagination and any resemblance to actual
people, places or events is coincidental or fictionalized.
Published in the United States by Clarkltd.
Po Box 45313 Rio Rancho, NM 87174
info@clarkltd.com

Edition 1

United States Copyright Office
#TX 8-387-676 April 2017
Library of Congress Control Number: 2017907164
International Standard Book Numbers
ISBN-10:099787676X
ISBN-13:978-0997876765
ASIN: B071YFKP4R

/200801

CONTENTS

ACKNOWLEDGMENTS

I dedicate this novel to my wonderful readers and for all the amazing people I've met and those I haven't. To my family and loved ones, all your support will not be forgotten.

This book was made possible by reviews from readers like you.

Thank you.

R.W.K. Clark

CHAPTER 1

It was a Tuesday. I had celebrated my birthday just three days before; my parents had given me a mountain bike, and it made me the envy of the few friends I had. I was still floating on Cloud 9, as a matter of fact. I was eager to take it out and show it off as soon as possible; there was no time to lose!

My best friend Travis and I had been hanging out at Grant Park, riding our bikes through it, over and over again, staring at the high school girls who were perfecting their tans over summer break. At twelve years old, both of us were getting pretty interested in their soft curves and silky curls, and we liked to spend time feasting our eyes as often as possible.

On this particular day, a trio of smoking hot babes showed up during our second ride through. We stopped at a picnic table across the lane from them, where they decided to bask; so we could enjoy the view all we wanted without creeping them out. We sat with our feet on the bench and our rears on the table top, and we whispered and giggled about what we would like to do to them if we were old enough. I was streaming our favorite music station on my cell phone, and we tapped our feet and bobbed our heads as we talked.

The clearest thing about that day to me was the normalcy of it. It's another day, just like any other; nothing could possibly go wrong today.

But then, the DJ interrupted the song and made an announcement: "Two ocean tankers carrying the newly developed mining chemical, 'IsoGold,' had collided in the Gulf of Mexico." The collision was so bad that every last drop of the stuff was leaked into the ocean. According to the report, everything would be fine. Scientists swore the stuff wasn't toxic, and they believed it would be easy to clean up. Lives were lost, but other than that, people had nothing to worry about. The spill wasn't threatening.

That evening at dinner my parents discussed it briefly, and they seemed a bit nervous as if they didn't want to talk about it in front of me. I didn't let it wear on me, and I went to bed and slept peacefully all through the night. But when I woke up the next morning my parents were both standing in front of the television, their attention focused on a news report about the spill. They looked a little worried, so I began to watch and listen as well.

A newscaster was speaking, but the screen was filled with footage taken from a helicopter. The water in the area of the spill was bubbling, and it had changed to a variety of colors. Dead sea life floated all around, and the carcasses of newly dead fish and animals popped up sporadically. In the distance, the waters appeared to still be blue, but on camera, I could see the colors and bubbles spreading, even as the man spoke.

He was saying that no one in the general vicinity was able to drink the water—that at the rate the spill was spreading, it was going to take over completely, and it was causing panic and hysteria. While reassurances were made that the scientific community was working to rectify the problem, they also realized that the 'harmless' IsoGold chemical wasn't at all harmless once it touched the water.

At that very second, I felt something inside of me change. I didn't know what it was I felt. All I knew was that the sensation was much like something snapping inside my chest. I learned about the ecosystem and the cycle of life, and how the two go hand in hand. I didn't understand all that was happening or most of what the reporter was saying. But I could understand the floating dead bodies of sea life... Something very, very bad was happening.

Governments all around the world began distributing bottled water immediately, but that didn't last. All attempts to clean existing water failed, and soon an electrolyte-based liquid was developed for us to both drink and bathe in. The result was AquaSim, a man-made water replacement. It wasn't intended for the long-term, but it would sustain us until the necessary improvements could be made. For a long time there was no swimming, no carefree trips to lakes or rivers; and in some parts of the world, people were dying as a direct result of the spill.

It spread like wildfire. It spread so fast that by the

end of the first year there wasn't a body of water that had not been affected. Another thing that spread just as quickly was the sick fad of cruising the waters to gawk at the deadly, however, beautiful—boiling and bubbling that IsoGold caused.

It's been four years now since the chemical created to make mining for gold easier and more efficient, robbed us of one of the very things that gave us life and health.

It stole our water.

∞

The sea had always been at the top of my list of favorite places to visit. Any of the oceans, it didn't matter. The array of sea life and the beautiful underwater environments were enough to boggle my mind at every occasion.

My dad and mom have taken me to the ocean several times in my life. It had been the best when I was younger: the colors, sounds, and experiences underwater were always everything I could hope for them to be. All three of us loved to go scuba diving, but it had been a while since we were able to indulge in our favorite pastime because everything was different now.

I clearly remember being so influenced by our diving expeditions that I had wholeheartedly wanted to be a marine biologist when I grew up. When I was younger, I would chatter on and on about being a 'fish doctor,' and I wanted to work hard to keep the water clean for all of its inhabitants.

I had to chuckle as I thought back about my dream

of helping the ocean, it was a fond memory of a small boy with lofty dreams; heck, I'm only sixteen now. No. I may have been chuckling, but I was feeling bitter. The waters of Earth are nothing like they used to be; it made me want to cry then, and it makes me want to cry as I write this. It really pisses me off.

I shifted around in my chair. It's a hard, blue, metal and acrylic one that can be found on any deck of the ship, scattered here and there, offering a place for passengers to sit and reflect over what was now referred to worldwide as 'The Heavenly Waters.' The oceans and seas are not called this because of their wondrous blue color; they were nicknamed this for the orange and purple bubbles that surface and pop through the yellow water. The idiots of Earth seem to believe that the poisonous beauty everyone flocks to see is right up there visually with the galaxy, or at least the pictures of it we've all seen in textbooks and such. It's sick.

Sitting there on the patio of our stateroom, watching the passengers flock to the railings below, snapping photos and 'oohing' and 'aahing,' I felt nauseous. I didn't want to sit on the patio anymore. I didn't think I could take another second of the blinding 'beauty' of the chemical-filled waters that used to be the western Caribbean. My stomach was in a knot.

My parents' names are James and Katherine, but they go by Jim and Kate. They had left a half-hour before to attend a 'twilight' photography class. The waters are best photographed at night, due to the fact that the bright colors appear glowing almost neon. The truth is that the water does glow, or at least the poisons in it do. Anyway, my mom and dad's hobby for the last couple of years has been taking pictures of the water, so we often went on cruises to capture it's "beauty."

There was plenty for me to do on board if I wanted to. It was only the first night of our cruise, and I knew I'd better come to grips with spending two weeks here. A movie theater and several shows were going on, a juice bar where the kids my age liked to hang out. I could even go have a burger if I wanted, but my parents always made me attend meals with them, and we had eaten before their photo class. The restaurant we ate in was called 'The Grande,' and it was pretty fancy, with a staunch dress code: men have to wear a coat and tie, and women must wear evening dresses. My parents always had food that was hard to identify by just looking at it. That evening I had chicken alfredo, along with about three buttered pieces of Italian bread. I was stuffed, so the seafood remained nothing but the pipe dream of a growing adolescent boy.

I glanced at the digital clock on top of the dark flat-screen television: seven-forty-two. Mom and Dad wouldn't be back for nearly two hours, and that would only be a 'stop in,' as Mom called them. They would basically poke their heads in, ask if I was okay, and then leave to meet their cruise buddies, Rick, and Linda Roth. They would all have drinks and take in a late show before stumbling to bed. They had to get plenty of rest so they could do it all again tomorrow.

The Roths had one daughter, Julia, but she was in

college and didn't attend the cruises with her parents. I think she studied cello at Julliard or something. She was really good-looking, but she's got one of those snobby attitudes that makes it difficult for people to get comfortable around her. The way she sneered slightly when she looked at you always made you feel like everything you did stemmed from your obvious idiocy. To put it simply, she was stuck up, and I was glad she hadn't come. I would have been forced to be cordial, and being cordial was nearly impossible when it came to Julia Roth. Thinking of her always kind of struck a funny bone with me; there had been a time my parents flung around the loose idea that perhaps we would marry someday. She was a year or two older than I, so they liked to entertain the idea. Ha! That was never going to happen.

I finally decided that I couldn't take much more of the monotony or silence which our large stateroom offered. I didn't want to watch a movie; I didn't feel like visiting the video arcade. But I did want some air, maybe even someone to talk to. I thought maybe I would just stroll the decks; maybe I would come across something interesting enough to pass the time and entertain me other than the boiling sea.

I grabbed a jacket from the back of the door leading to my sleeping quarters and put it on as I left. Making sure I had the stateroom key, I made my way out of there and didn't look back. Soon enough I would have to return so my mom could make her 'stop in' and see that I was alive. For now, I had a couple of hours to pass, so I was determined to make them entirely mine.

CHAPTER 2

I am not the kind of person to have a lot of close friends. Back home in Chicago I'm acquainted with more people than I can count: people from school and people from my neighborhood. Most people I associate with call me by my first name, Tripp. I've gotten a lot of flak from my peers because of my name. Anyway, the point is that I really don't know very few people, and if I am familiar with them, we're merely on a first name basis.

I have only one close friend, Travis Bonser. We have been friends since he moved to Chicago in the first grade. He calls me 'Tripp the Drip.' I guess you could say, in many ways, we are like brothers. I had always wanted him to come on a cruise with us, just like he had gone scuba diving once with my family before. But since the water became sick his parents wouldn't let him go. They didn't want to put their only son at risk, sending him out into the middle of the filthy, dirty sea. I can't say that I blame them, but I always missed him during these cruises. I remember one time, right after the spill, Travis was supposed to go with us for our first 'new sea' cruise. His parents put their foot down so fast the ground shook. His mom blew up at mine, telling her it was a sick thing to take a family vacation to gawk at the poisonous and polluted ocean. The two never spoke again. If any communication was required, it took place between our fathers.

My decision to leave the stateroom and explore the ship turned out to be a good one. I immediately felt a rush as I stepped into the corridor and observed all the other passengers who were milling about; the place was a madhouse. Little kids were darting here and there, laughing and hollering. One little girl was sprawled out on the floor, kicking and screaming while her mom struggled to open the door to their stateroom. Most of the adults were standing at the rails, pouring all of their attention into the waters below. Some were snapping pictures, others were discussing its appearance in either heated tones or hushed whispers. Almost everyone seemed to be in awe of its deceptively beautiful colors, and swirls distracted dumbly by its horrific nature.

I decided I would take the elevator to the highest deck. I wanted to get an eyeful of the sea from there, and then go to the next lower deck to do the same. Maybe, in the process, I would figure out something else to do to pass the time until Mom and Dad got back to the stateroom. The 'Diamond of the Sea' was a massive ship. It consisted of sixteen passenger-accessible decks. Most of the floors were made up of staterooms and cabins, but five or six of them were loaded with restaurants, boutiques, game rooms, theaters, bars… the list goes on. For a newbie, it can be an overwhelming place. A small floating city.

I thought about checking out the arcade. I had been into gaming for a while, even to the point where I got sort of strung out on it if you know what I mean. But, as soon as I saw how it was affecting my grades, I did what I had to and walked away. Now, I have acquaintances who didn't make that choice, didn't man up. They let an electronic box ruin their futures, and they couldn't keep up with school. Mind-blowing, but true.

I pushed any thoughts of the arcade out of my mind. Just getting some air and looking at the stars sounded awesome for the time being. If I cleared my head, I'd be able to make a decision much faster. I walked up behind several people who were waiting for the elevator; both 'up' and 'down' had been called, so I waited with them. After what seemed like forever, the doors opened. That was the second I saw the most beautiful girl I had ever seen in my life, she was getting off the elevator right before my very eyes.

She walked like a dream. It seemed like she was surrounded by a light from heaven, and it nearly blinded me. She appeared to almost float as she stepped out of the elevator and passed right by me, just inches from me, oblivious to my existence. Her dark red hair was thick and long, and her eyes were a light, powdery blue; the sight of her made my heart pound and my palms wet. I tried to open my mouth to say 'hi,' but it was so dry that I couldn't even peel my tongue off the roof of my mouth effectively enough to spit anything out.

But then, a miracle! Just before she had passed me completely, she turned, looked straight at me, and offered me a shy smile. I began to shake like crazy as my eyes followed her. Before I knew it, she was caught up in the crowd, and she was gone.

I must have stood there, my mouth hanging open, for an hour. At least, it seemed like that long. I was jostled out of my reverie by the people shoving past me to get on the elevator; yes, the elevator I had missed. When reality hit me, I pulled myself together quickly and managed to elbow my way onto the next available car.

Even on the ride up, and through each stop, I could feel that my face was flushed, and I had to drag my palms along the legs of my jeans in an effort to dry them off more than once. My eyes darted nervously over the other people in the elevator; I was hoping my nervous state wasn't obvious to strangers, but no one seemed to notice. I breathed a sigh of relief.

By this point, it was truly a relief to discover that the top deck had a low level of activity going on. There were a few other passengers: a couple who were swooning over each other, and a few other kids about my age down at the other end. In between were random people enjoying the outside weather. The deck chairs were pretty empty; I guess people wanted to see the pollution in the water on an up-close-and-personal basis. Sick.

Of course, I immediately avoided the couple. It was always best to be courteous and offer privacy in these situations. My father had taught me that way back when, so I didn't even really have to think about it. I gave them a single glance, registered their presence and appearance, and made a beeline for the rail. Might as well get a look while I was up here.

For me personally, the sea looked better from higher up. You could see the colors, but it was much more difficult to observe the bubbling and boiling from that high up, so it simply seemed that colored lights from the ship were reflecting off the water. For a second it seemed like the water was back to normal, and it made something in my heart ache.

A kid with a baseball cap passed by and caught my eye. He acknowledged me with a half-nod of his head; then he pushed the button for the elevator. I looked back over the rail, but then I heard the elevator door open and close, so I looked up and saw that two other guys he had been with were still down at the other end. They, too, were looking over the rail. They were talking and pointing, and occasionally one of them would laugh. I slowly started in their direction.

"It almost looks alluring from up here, eh, guys?" I asked as I neared them.

Both of them jerked their heads in my direction, the smiles disappearing from their faces. I stopped so they could look me over, and I must have passed the inspection. After a brief moment, the kid on the left, who was stockier and taller than his companion, offered me a smile.

"Yeah, I guess it does," he replied. "What's up,

dude?"

I offered him a shrug and joined them at the rail, leaving a good three feet between us. "My parents bring me on these cruises all the time. Guess I get sick of treating poison water like a day at the museum, you know what I mean?"

They were both silent for a moment, then he told me, "Yeah. I see your point. My name's Drake; this is Mike. Feel free to call him 'Mikey.'"

"Heck with you," Mike spat. "Mike is fine, thank you."

It turned out that both Drake and Mike were from Michigan. Drake's parents were both doctors, and they cruised twice a year, just like my folks. They always made Drake go with them. This year he had talked them into letting Mike join in so he wouldn't be so bored. Same story, different family, I guess.

Their exchange made me smile. "I'm Tripp."

Mike turned to me and studied my face. "Tripp?" he asked.

"I know, right?"

The three of us chuckled, and I endured a 'Tripp on a trip' joke before we turned our attention back to the waters below. We were quiet for a moment. As I would soon learn, Drake was the talker of the two.

"Ya know," he began. "I'm sittin' here and watchin' all these people act like they are looking at one of the seven wonders or somethin'." He shook his head. "I don't think I'll ever get it, no matter how many times my parents drag me on these stupid cruises. How do you celebrate this kind of destruction? Don't these people realize that this is the beginning of the end?"

I listened to him intently. He continued on about how it used to feel to take a dip in a lake or to actually drink fresh, cold water instead of the bottled, lab-created electrolyte drinks that we had now. I could remember all of the same things, as could a sullen, nodding Mike.

I knew the other two would agree: the world was definitely on its way to dismay, and people were paying for the trip and flocking to board the boat.

R.W.K. Clark

CHAPTER 3

I ended up hanging out with Mike and Drake until it was time for me to head back to the stateroom. The three of us were very close in age and had a lot in common. Mike was fifteen and would turn sixteen in two months. Drake would be seventeen soon. I fell right in the middle. We talked about high school and what we wanted to study in college. We talked about girls, and I told them about the sweet angel of a redhead who had blinded me earlier. Neither of them knew who she was, but they promised to keep their eyes out.

In retrospect, I can tell you that Drake liked to come off as sort of a dumb jock. I didn't know why, and I never asked. All I knew was that he was smart; it would slip out from beneath his oafish façade every now and then. I think maybe he was trying to keep himself on his best friend, Mike's, level. Mike was a bit dim; perhaps similarly, he behaved the way he did for his pal's sake.

∞

The next thing I knew it was morning, and I was having breakfast with my mother and father. Dad had managed to really tie one on with the Roths the night before and decided he didn't want to dine at the restaurant, so we had food brought to the stateroom. French toast, bagels, scrambled eggs, western hashed browns, and our choice of bacon, sausage, or ham. I had a tall cold milk, but both of my parents were sipping on Bloody Marys, and they had the curtains drawn against the sunlight. Must have done a bit too much celebrating with the Roths last night, I figured.

My dad was fairly quiet as we ate. He kept his eyes on the television news, and he only gave an occasional grunt in response to what he was hearing. Mom asked me about my evening. I told her about Drake and Mike, which interested her greatly because I was not one to go out and make 'pals,' as she called them. But when I told her how disgusted we all were with how people treated the polluted seas, she quickly lost interest. No one likes to feel like they lack moral character, and I couldn't seem to reconcile moral character with the celebration of destruction. When I noticed her attention waning, I stopped talking and cleaned my plate in a hurry.

"I'm going to meet those guys, and we're going to check out the ship," I said as I put my plate on the food cart and went to the bathroom to brush my teeth. I heard my mom give me a slight 'mm-hmm' in response, so I closed the bathroom door and went about my business.

About thirty seconds later I heard a loud knock at the stateroom door. I came out of the bathroom just as my mother opened it. One of the ship's stewards stood in the corridor, a plastic smile on his face.

"Mrs. Young?"

"Yes," my mother replied. "How can I help you? We're not quite done with breakfast here, but if you come back –"

The young man shook his head. "No, ma'am. I'm here for another reason, unfortunately. It seems that a child has gone missing on the ship. We are going from stateroom to stateroom to ask if anyone has seen the child." Immediately he produced a color copy of what appeared to be a school photo.

The girl in the photo looked to be seven or eight years old. She had long blond hair and a face like a little pixie. Her eyes were large and brown, and she had perfect little teeth. She smiled as if she didn't have a care in the world, and I realized that, at that age, she probably didn't.

"Her name is Sarah Mills. We're sure she is just wandering around somewhere," he continued. "Her parents are frantic."

My mother and father, stared at the picture with squinted eyes as they tried to place the child. I stood behind them and did the same. After a moment, I realized we were all shaking our heads as we stared.

"No," my mom said. "No, I don't think so."

My father interjected. "But we will certainly keep our eyes out!" I agreed with him.

"Thank you," the steward concluded. "We will keep everyone posted with updates."

When he had left, my mother stated with a sad voice, "That's horrible. I can't imagine. I hope she didn't fall into the water! Tripp, you keep your eyes out for that child today, all right?"

"Absolutely." I tended to agree with the steward, though. She was likely just exploring.

I don't know if I was aware of it right away or not, but the picture of that kid got to me. How do you lose a kid on a cruise ship? I hoped something bad hadn't happened. It had me a bit anxious, and I knew that no matter what the guys and I decided to do, I would have an eye out for little Sarah Mills.

∞

Fifteen minutes later I was sitting on the upper deck with Drake and Mike, and we were discussing the circumstances and tossing around theories.

"That kid and her parents are in the stateroom right next to us," Drake was informing me. "She has an older brother, too. Anyway, I heard her parents talking to mine in the hall this morning, and they said that Sarah had been playing hide and seek along one of the decks. She went to hide, and they couldn't find her; she never came back."

"Maybe she's in a lifeboat or something, fast asleep," I offered.

Both Drake and Mike nodded, then Drake continued. "I'm sure they will check every lifeboat there is. They said that if they don't find her by the time the noon hour is over they are going to search stateroom to stateroom. Crazy, huh?"

Yeah, it was crazy, but she couldn't have gone too far on an ocean liner. Well, I guess she could have fallen overboard, but it was a terrible thought, and I didn't even want to think about that. Honestly, the thought made me want to cry, and I didn't want to look like a sissy in front of these guys.

"I keep looking for that cute ginger from the elevator I told you about last night." I grinned as I changed the subject. "I'd sure like a chance to talk to her."

Mike guffawed. "You wanna do more than that with her!"

"Yeah, yeah."

"We know, Trippy," Drake chimed in. "You wanna marry her."

I shook my head, but I was amused. "Shut up, jerks. So, are we gonna check out this big heap of metal, or what?"

They both jumped up simultaneously as if they were a pair of puppets on the same string. We began to slouch away, walking with the ever famous 'teenage boy' gait and posture. I had to admit, I was anxious to explore a bit. It amazed even me how many times I had been on either this ship or one just like it, and I had never really gone 'exploring.' I'd never even been in to see the bridge!

Well, it seemed that today was the day to begin, and I had a couple of sidekicks to do it with. We were on Deck 16, which had a fitness center, an observation tower, and a SeaPlex, with tons of activities, as well as video gaming. It was the third day of a two-week cruise so we would have plenty to do and see, that was for sure.

I'll be honest when I tell you, that in the beginning, we were going to just sort of 'skim' over the top deck, but when we entered the SeaPlex, all bets were off. We walked in intending to just do a 'stroll through,' but we weren't in the doors ten seconds when I saw her.

She was standing with a group of three other girls, all around her age. She was smiling, but the smile didn't touch her eyes. To be honest, she looked like she felt about as uncomfortable as she possibly could, the way I feel much of the time.

As soon as I saw her, I froze. I felt my mouth drop open, and my heartbeat picked up. Drake and Mike just kept walking, unaware that I was stuck right where I had stopped. Soon they had turned around, saw me standing there dumbfounded, and walked back to me with stupid grins on their faces.

"What's the matter, dude?" Mike asked.

A cat had my tongue; all I could do was a nod in the direction of my dream lover.

Both of them looked. "Is that her?" Drake inquired, and I nodded stupidly.

"So, go talk to her," they both said at once.

I shook myself to gain control. "Naw. That's dumb. She is with a bunch of girls! Forget that; I'll pass."

Now we were all three staring. "She is cute," Drake mumbled.

"Yeah, she is," Mike muttered. "You gotta go talk to her, man. If you don't, one of us might."

I glanced at Mike to my left, then Drake to my right. Both of them were practically drooling. Yeah, she was cute. I knew that if I didn't make some kind of move one of these clowns was going to jump at the chance. I took a deep breath and squared my shoulders.

"All right. I'm gonna do it."

Drake had started to breathe through his mouth. "Go for it, man. We're right here for ya."

I closed my eyes, inhaled deeply once again, then took the first step. When I opened them, she was standing there with her arms crossed, smiling politely while her friends laughed at some unknown joke. Slowly, I made my way in her direction.

As I neared her, I could see she was far more beautiful than I had first thought. Her skin was like porcelain: natural, white, and flawless, except for the perfect tiny smattering of freckles across her nose, almost like a light powdering. I could feel my hands trembling as I got closer and closer. When I was about five feet from her, she noticed me approaching, and her smile began to grow.

But then disaster struck. I wasn't two feet from her when, out of nowhere, some little kid rolled a tennis ball across the floor. I didn't see it coming at all; Drake filled me in after. Anyway, my foot came right down on it, rolling on the ball and throwing me into the air. I landed hard on my back with a loud 'Ooof!' The impact knocked the wind right out of me.

The first thing I heard was an explosion of feminine laughter. I lay there, so embarrassed I was sure I would die and listened with a broken heart and closed eyes.

"Oh, man!" Mike and Drake were next to me then,

pulling me off the floor and to my feet. "I can't believe you fell in front of those girls, man!"

Once I was standing, I still had to gasp for breath, but I was pulling it together. I began to brush my butt off, and I let my eyes follow the girls as I did it. All of them were still laughing as they rolled their eyes and walked away, whispering and pointing. But I'll tell you this much: she wasn't laughing! She was smiling, and she was looking me right in the eye. I have to admit, it was a very flirtatious smile, too.

"Just shoot me now," I said when they were out of earshot. I put my face in my hands and shook my head. I could feel the heat emanating from my cheeks.

Drake chuckled. "I know, right? That's a bummer. Well, it's early in the trip, Tripp. You'll get another chance. Now, let's go check out the surf machine. You guys are wearing suits under your jeans, right?"

The Flowrider was a surf machine on the ship. It used to use water, back in the day. Now it ran on a safe man-made liquid that had been developed for swimming and showering since the big dump first happened. You couldn't get it in your mouth, and you had to have plugged ears and goggled eyes, and it smelled like chemicals, but if you played it safe, it wouldn't kill you. You might get some kind of infection or wind up nursing flu-like symptoms for three days, but it wouldn't kill you. Funny. Because of those side effects, I didn't really feel like surfing, but I was willing to watch the guys if they wanted to.

So, that was what we did until lunch, then we went

our separate ways. We planned to meet up on Deck 16 and hit the arcade area for a while. On the way back to my stateroom I thought about the red-haired girl, and I hoped for another chance with her, as well as a lot more confidence.

R.W.K. Clark

CHAPTER 4

Lunch with the folks flew by with little to no pain. They told me they were going to an afternoon dance class with the Roths, and I told them that the guys and I were planning on gaming the afternoon away. I endured a lecture regarding video games, self-control, and knowing when to walk away, blah, blah, blah. Overall though, they seemed happy that I was hanging out with guys my own age and socializing instead of holing up in the stateroom all by myself.

All three of us left together, with solid plans to dress for dinner around five. I met up with Drake and Mike at the arcade, and in true teenage boy form, the three of us managed to waste the entire afternoon playing video games. It was heaven, and it ended too soon. I took comfort in the fact that it was only the third day on board.

∞

At six-thirty I was sitting at the restaurant in my stiff suit and tie, waiting for my éclair dessert and listening to my mom and dad talk about the missing girl, Sarah Mills. It turned out that no one had tracked her down yet, and her mother was in a deep state of grief and shock. According to my mom, word had it that the Coast Guard had begun searching the waters, while the ship search continued as well.

"They'll never actually stop the ship," she was saying with disgust. "I mean, can you imagine how many passengers would demand their money back if the cruise was stopped?"

My father grunted and took a drink.

"I would," she continued. "You can bet I would either get my money back or get a free cruise."

The conversation was disgusting. "Mom."

"What, Tripp?" she asked, her voice full of confusion. "Paying customers deserve to get their money's worth or to have it made right." She turned to my father. "Don't you agree, dear?"

He grunted again.

"Mother, we are talking about a little girl!" I exclaimed. "Wouldn't you want the boat to stop if it were me?"

She stared blankly at me for a moment, then said, "But they won't stop the ship for such a thing."

It was my turn to stare now, and I was doing it in disbelief. Did I really come from these two people?

"Excuse me," I muttered. I tossed my napkin in the middle of my plate and left the table before they had a chance to stop me.

∞

I got changed as fast as I could, so as to not run into my parental units, then I made my way to Deck 15, where the theater was located. There was some new comic book hero movie we had wanted to see, though I can't remember the name of it now to save my life. I hadn't been to a movie with friends in two years since Travis and I went and saw the millionth Superhuman remake.

Mike and Drake were waiting for me as promised. There were a ton of kids, my age and younger, as well as some young adults, milling around, waiting to get in and sit down. I approached the guys, slapping Mike on the shoulder when I reached them.

"Good dinner I hope?" I began. "Mine wasn't. Did you know they haven't found that missing girl yet?" Drake stated. "My mom said the Coast Guard is involved, but they don't plan on stopping the boat. It's bull, I tell ya."

Both Drake and Mike nodded in agreement. Drake said with a sneer, "Yeah, and even if they find any sign of her in the water, it will be nothing but floating bones. The water would have eaten her skin right off."

"She probably didn't even know what hit her," Mike chimed in. "Probably killed the poor kid right away."

Suddenly, Drake swung his arm and slapped my shoulder hard. I jumped, and my hand went right to the spot and began to rub it. "What did you do that for?" I asked.

He smiled and motioned with his head. "Isn't that her?"

My stinging shoulder was forgotten as I looked in the intended direction. Yes, there she was, standing and waiting with another girl. But this time she was already staring at me, and she was smiling. My stomach did a flip as I watched her say something to her friend and wave coyly at me. After a few seconds, she began to walk in my direction.

"Oh, man," I stammered. "She's coming over here! What should I do?"

Mike and Drake exchanged teasing glances, and Mike said, "Well, I guess ya better talk to her, moron."

I didn't have time to debate. In a fraction of a second, she was standing there, right in front of me, smiling. "Hey, guys. Looking forward to the movie?"

"Yeah," my friends said in unison; I was incapable of speech, it seemed.

She continued to wait for my answer, and when she realized my mouth was stuck, she continued. "I'm Heidi. Heidi Collins."

My pals mumbled their names before Drake reached out and punched me in the arm to try to get my speech going. "Uh, hi," I finally said as blood rushed into my cheeks. "I'm Tripp... Young."

"Tripp?" she asked, her smile growing. I braced myself for the obligatory teasing, but she surprised me. "That's a cool name. You don't hear that much."

Her friend, a chubby brown-haired girl with glasses, sidled up beside her. "Come on Heidi!"

Heidi didn't even look at her. "Tripp here asked me to join him. Hope that's okay, Jennifer."

All three of us guys exchanged glances as we recognized her fib, but we said nothing.

"Oh," Jennifer said. "Well, that's fine. I'll find my

brother. See you after, okay?"

Jennifer trotted off, and when she was out of hearing distance, Heidi said, "Thanks. I don't really have a lot in common with her, or any of my friends on this boat for that matter. I only know them through my parents... anyway, do you mind if I sort of tag along with you guys for the show?"

I could feel both Drake and Mike watching me, waiting for me to be the one to give a response. It seemed that words were still eluding me, so I just shook my head to let her know it was fine. As far as I was concerned my pals could have joined Jennifer and let me and Heidi be. I'd trudge my way through the waters of shyness on my own.

With that, we all made our way into the theater and found four seats closer to the back. As we got comfortable, Heidi, who was sitting next to me on the end, leaned over and said to us, "So, isn't it crazy about that little girl? Have you heard? I can't believe they aren't stopping the cruise. My dad said that if her parents want off they have to be picked up by helicopter, but they won't leave until she is found anyway."

"Does your family know them?" I asked, seemingly able to suddenly speak normally.

Heidi nodded her head. "Only my dad and he knows them because the guy works with him. It was my dad who talked them into coming to see the waters because he's someone they get grants from. He feels like all of this is his fault. My parents don't think she fell into the water though."

"Oh, yeah?" Drake interrupted. "Why not?"

"Well," she replied in a 'matter of fact' tone, "my dad is a marine biologist. Since there isn't any sea life anymore, he studies the water. He said if she fell overboard her body would have just lain on top of the water, sort of floating and melting. He said she would have died fast, because the poison would have soaked into her pores, but that her body would take a bit of time to melt. He says the Coast Guard would have found her right away if she went over the rail, or at least recognized it as human remains."

The lights went down then, and the movie screen lit up. Previews began to play, so we all sat back and tried to focus on the movie. I had a hard time, though. All I could think about was a dead little girl floating on the tainted water, melting as the chemicals dissolved her flesh. It made me sick.

I couldn't even keep up with the movie. The special effects were the best part, and that wasn't saying much.

By the time it was over I was so relieved to just get up and get out of that place. I wanted some air; it seemed so hot and stuffy, and I still couldn't get the thought of that missing girl out of my mind. If she was on board, why couldn't they find her? Why wouldn't they stop the ship?

Back on deck, I took great gulps of air. It lessened the sickness in my stomach and cleared my head. The four of us stood there for a minute, looking expectantly at each other. Suddenly, Heidi had become a bit shy.

"So, uh, thanks for letting me hang with you guys," she began.

I shifted my weight from one foot to the other nervously. "Sure. No problem."

I looked over at Drake and Mike, who were staring at me and grinning. I would get to hear about my little crush from them, I was sure. Maybe I could postpone it for a bit.

"Do you want me to walk you to your stateroom?" I asked.

Heidi shrugged. "What are you guys gonna do?"

Another glance at the boys told me that they didn't care if she hung out. I suspected they wanted something to razz me about, and having her with us would give them plenty of ammunition. To be honest, I didn't want to walk her back to her stateroom. I could bask in her glory for days.

"We were just gonna grab a soda and hang out on the upper deck if you want to stick around." I started to fidget. "I can walk you back whenever you like. No problem."

Heidi's eyes lit up, and she flashed an award-winning smile. "Awesome!"

So, with shaking hands, I got sodas for both Heidi and myself, and while we waited for the guys to order theirs, we had our first chance to talk alone.

"So, Tripp," she began, "where are you from?"

I took a swallow of my cola. "Chicago. You?"

"Miami Beach," she replied. "Like I don't get enough of the toxic views during my daily life, so my

35

parents have to bring me on these cruises. Are you a 'drag along' like me?"

I laughed and nodded. "Yeah. The way people almost worship this contaminated crap is beyond me."

"Right?"

"This is the last year I'm going to come, though," I continued. "It gets worse and worse, and my mom and dad are, like, obsessed with it. I told them when we left this time that I wasn't coming after this."

"That's too bad," she said. "So, this might be, like, the only time I ever see you?"

I shrugged, and I could feel myself blushing once again. "I guess. But I suppose it doesn't have to be."

"Doesn't have to be what?" Drake interjected. Drake and Mike were suddenly back, and I found myself wishing that I didn't embarrass so easily.

"Nothing," Heidi said, saving the moment. "So, let's head up. You wanna take the stairs since it's only a deck away?"

Drake cleared his throat. "You know, I have a little headache, so I think Mike and I are going to head to the stateroom and hit the sack. You two kids have fun, okay?"

I felt a flood of relief. More time alone with Heidi! One look at Drake told me that the headache was trumped up; he was trying to give me some space to work some magic. What kind of magic? I had no idea; I was sixteen and pretty straight-laced.

"We'll meet up tomorrow, Tripp, all right?" he said.

With that, it was settled. In minutes, Heidi and I

were on Deck 16 pulling a couple of deck chairs together so we could hang out and look at whatever stars we could see in the sky.

"What do your parents do?" she asked.

I cringed at the question. I wasn't especially proud of my parents' careers. I groaned a bit before telling her that my father was president of a chemical and pharmaceutical company (a contributor to the Earth's problems) and my mother was a lawyer for the same. But I still love them, even though they were both at the bottom of the professional ethics totem pole. I ended my short, fairly mellow rant by simply saying, "I hate it; it's embarrassing."

Heidi listened in silence and didn't respond right away. Instead, she took my hand and just held it. The gesture was quite possibly one of the most meaningful things anyone had ever done for me, and I fell in love that very second. Suddenly, Heidi was no longer a crush; I was going to marry her. I lay back on my deck chair, next to her, and we just held hands in silence for a while.

It was heaven, and I couldn't believe it was happening to me.

You see, I was never the boy in school who had girls flocking to him. I'm good-looking enough, don't get me wrong. I have light brown hair, which I wear pretty long, and hazel eyes. I'm five-foot-eleven, and because I participate in extra-curricular sports at school and work out a little in the summer, I have a good physique. But I'm not a 'bad boy,' and girls seem to like 'bad boys.'

The band members and motorcycle riders… you know the like. I'm kind of a dork, a nerd. I read, I love to learn, and I'm a thinker. The contrast is not always beneficial to drawing in the ladies, believe me.

After a short while, she pulled me out of my head. "My dad actually wants to fight the pollution. He works pretty hard trying to find a way to clean the water up. That's the reason we come on these cruises. I guess I was raised to hate it just like my parents. I can't imagine feeling that way and then living with people who contribute to it. I'm sorry, Tripp."

"Don't be sorry," I replied softly. "It helps me identify the kind of person I don't want to be."

I could feel her eyes studying my face, and I wondered what she was thinking. Maybe it made her sick that my parents were the way they were. Maybe she was looking at me and thinking, 'how could I have been interested in a polluter?' But she didn't let go of my hand, and I let that fact do all the talking. If I made her sick, she would certainly be letting go, wouldn't she?

At last, she broke the silence. "Isn't it crazy about that little girl? What's her name? Sarah something, I think."

"Mills," I replied. "And it is crazy; it's been in the back of my mind, nagging, ever since I first found out. So, your dad really doesn't think she could have gone overboard, huh?"

Heidi turned her attention back to the stars. "Nope. He says that if we came into direct contact with the water, in the state it's in, we would die right away, and that we would just float on top of it. When all our skin was gone, our bones would keep floating, in the same position we died in and everything."

"That's nuts," I mused.

"Right?" she said, then she paused and continued. "He thinks she is somewhere on the ship like she's lost, or someone snatched her. He wanted to help look for her, but the ship's crew won't let the passengers look anywhere except in places they are supposed to be. I still can't believe they didn't stop the cruise as soon as she came up missing."

I thought about that, and about how my mother had shown so much denial and shock at the very thought. "I just don't understand how all these people think. They stroll around and stare at the water, taking pictures and ogling over it. They all know what it means, but they turn it into a big adventure. Ugh."

Heidi sat up on her deck lounger and turned toward me. "I think these cruises should be illegal. That's what I think."

I looked up at her. The lights from the deck were shining behind her head, making her look almost unrealistically pretty, like a drawing. She seemed so soft and delicate; how could she be interested in me?

"I would have to say that's the best idea I've heard in a while," I replied in a still, soft voice.

She reclined once again, still holding onto my hand, and I turned my attention back to the moon and stars. I let my thoughts turn to the spill, the event which forever changed life as all of us knew it here on planet

Earth. The event that would ultimately and certainly spell out our demise.

CHAPTER 5

"So, how did it go last night?" Mike asked.

It was just after ten the following morning, and Drake, Mike, and I were walking around the ship, exploring. We had decided that we would head up to the running track on Deck 15; to watch the women jog.

The question Drake asked almost made me blush. I knew I wouldn't get out of giving some kind of report, so I gave in. After all, it wasn't like I had to tell them everything.

"It was good," I replied. "To be honest, we really didn't do much. We hung out on Deck 16 and watched the stars and the moon."

Mike spoke up. "Did you do it?"

I slugged him in the arm. "No, and even if I did, I wouldn't tell you."

The truth was that we held hands the entire time, and then I walked her to her stateroom and gave her a peck on the cheek. I didn't believe in disrespect, and I didn't want her to feel like I wanted only one thing. I was really into Heidi.

I put up with their razzing all the way to the track, thinking that they would let up once the jogging girls had their attention. But as soon as we arrived the first jogger to come into sight was none other than Heidi herself. Of course, their snickers and comments increased until she saw us and sped up to reach us faster. Let them have their fun, I figured. I was the one getting her attention.

"Hi, Tripp," she greeted me as the four of us made our way to a row of deck chairs outside the fitness center. The seats afforded my two friends ample rear-views of the joggers, most of whom were female. Soon, they had their eyes glued to the passing women, their heads going from the right to the left like reverse bobbleheads. At last, Heidi and I had a chance to talk.

"Guess what?" she began. "This morning at breakfast my father told me that Sarah Mills is not in the ocean. They ruled out drowning. Then, he was talking to our waiter about it, and he said that one report said she was last seen playing hide and seek with a group of kids while her parents were photographing the water. I guess she ran to hide, and that was the last time she was seen by anyone."

"Drake overheard her mom and dad telling his parents the same thing," I replied. "I'm sure they searched that deck thoroughly, I mean down to every bolt and nut, don't you think?"

Yes, I was sure they had, but the second mention of this fact got my mind racing immediately. What if the girl had hidden in a tight space and been unable to get out? What if she was still trapped there, hungry and crying? After all, if Heidi's dad was right—considering his profession I was sure he was—then the girl had to be somewhere on the ship.

I turned to Heidi, my eyes lit up with a bit of excitement. "Maybe we should look for her ourselves," I whispered.

Heidi flashed me a grin and nodded. "That's what I thought, too. We couldn't let anyone know, though. They have the ship's crew and a ton of adults helping; they would say we are in the way. We would have to act like we were doing regular stuff, you know, and just poke around whenever the coast is clear."

I reached across Heidi and poked Drake in the arm. "Hey, did you hear what Heidi said? That missing girl was last seen playing hide and seek. That's the report the ship has. We want to look for her. Are you game?"

He offered Heidi a brief glance, then said, "Sure. You think she is stuck somewhere from hiding, huh?"

"Makes sense, doesn't it?" I replied.

He nodded. "She was last seen on Deck 3, from what her mom said."

"According to the report," Heidi whispered, picking up where Drake left off, "the person who last saw her was some teenage girl. She claims she saw one little girl hiding her eyes and counting, and then she saw Sarah run from the entrance to the theater on that deck all the way down in the direction of the casinos until she was out of sight."

"A waiter told you all this?" Drake asked, and Heidi just nodded, a stubborn, sure look on her face.

"Won't they be searching there right now?" Mike

asked.

Heidi shook her head. "This waiter said they already searched Deck 3 thoroughly, and they expect to find her on another. They are working their way up; really that's all they can do if they aren't going to stop and get help from the law."

In my mind, the issue was settled. "So, I say we start on Deck 3 and work our way up, the same as they are," I offered.

With head-nods all around, the four of us got to our feet and headed for the elevators. We likely wouldn't find her, but I certainly wanted to give it a try. She could be tucked away in a place they just overlooked. At least, that was my hope.

Deck 3 consisted of staterooms, a couple of restaurants, a casino, a large theater, and a bunch of seating. The elevator delivered us there quickly, and once we arrived, we stopped long enough to form a plan of action. We all agreed it was best to be somewhat organized.

Heidi and I would begin in and around the theater; Drake and Mike would start at the other end, and we would meet in the middle.

The theater had nothing playing right then, but the staff wouldn't allow us inside at first. Heidi made up a creative story about leaving her purse under a seat, saying she wasn't sure which one, and that was enough for the guy in charge to tell us to 'go ahead, and make it quick.' We went through the place, searching under each and every seat, but no luck. We even peeked out of the emergency exits, to no avail.

Next, we gave the deck around the theater a good going-over, then headed toward the elevators, stairs, and casino. The bathrooms were there, and I told Heidi I was going to take a break while she looked the area over. That was when everything started to go crazy.

I just left the men's room and was passing by the stairs when Heidi gave a shrill scream. I jumped and looked to the left; she was kneeling on the floor beneath the stairs, her back to me. I ran to her thinking she was hurt, and as soon as I reached her, I dropped to my knees to help. That was when I saw it.

Heidi had a small, hatch-type door open beneath the stairs. The first thing I saw was the water, which seemed to cover the floor inside the compartment she was looking into. It was bright orange, and green bubbles boiled to the surface, even as it pooled on the compartment floor. I remember thinking, for just a second, that it was alive, that it had to be alive to do the things it was doing.

Then I saw the solid red streaks swirling here and there all through the puddle. Heidi threw herself into my arms and buried her face in my neck. She was sobbing uncontrollably. I couldn't seem to understand why she was so upset. I continued to hold her while trying to focus my eyes in the gloom beneath the steps. I followed the red streaks, and that was when I saw the bones floating on the surface of the water, which was less than an inch deep. They were the bones of a small child, and they were floating perfectly in position as if the girl had unzipped her skin and lain down for a nap.

I held onto Heidi and just stared, my mouth agape in shock. I hadn't truly thought we would find her, and I had thought that she would be alive; shaken, but alive. I trembled like a leaf from my head to my feet, and my heart was pounding.

"We have to get help, Heidi," I said softly as I pulled her to her feet. "We have to find someone to get her out of there."

I began to walk toward a crew member who was conversing casually with a passenger, practically dragging Heidi with me as I went. I was moving as quickly as possible, the man glanced toward me, then turned his full attention to us as soon as he got a look at the hysterical Heidi. He raced to us, concern all over his face.

"Is she okay?" he asked. "What happened?"

I sat my sobbing partner down in a deck chair and turned to the man, whose chest tag read 'Kip Reeves, steward.' "You have to come with me!"

Maybe it was the tone of my voice, or perhaps it was the look on my face, but when I turned to lead the way Kip Reeves didn't hesitate. "Is she going to be all right?" he asked.

"Yeah, just come on," I replied, and broke into a slight jog, which he immediately emulated.

When we reached the staircase, I knelt down right away, and I pointed into the compartment, which was still wide open. Reeves knelt down as well, and suddenly he gasped loudly. I turned to observe a panic-stricken look on his face.

The steward grabbed his radio off his belt and began barking into it. I fell back onto the seat of my pants and just stared into the compartment. The shock was definitely catching up to me now. I was having a hard time breathing, and I could feel tears falling silently down my face. They felt hot enough to burn my skin.

"Why is there water in there?" I asked.

He didn't answer my question. "Come on. Your girlfriend needs you."

Chaos broke loose after that. The deck was evacuated, and another crew member escorted us to the deck above, where we found Drake and Mike waiting expectantly. I was holding Heidi again, and I just looked at them and told them we had to get her back to her room.

"What happened?" Drake asked as we began to walk.

I offered him a teary glance. "We found her, man. We found Sarah Mills."

Mike's eyes lit up. "That's great!"

I shook my head. "Just help me get her to her stateroom, guys."

The smiles disappeared from their faces. They realized that however, she was found, she wasn't alive. There was no way they could have imagined it at all. It had to be the single saddest thing to happen; to lose a child in such a manner.

Drake took Heidi by her other arm, and we began to make our way to the elevators as quickly as possible.

Soon, we were at her stateroom on Deck 11, and Mike was banging on the door. He was banging hard and continually, almost in sort of an anxious state himself. I think seeing Heidi cry uncontrollably had him feeling a bit out of sorts.

The door was quickly opened by an attractive woman with auburn hair and a bright smile, which faded as soon as she laid eyes on Heidi. "What happened?"

Her mother grabbed her at her armpits and struggled to steer her inside, with all three of us boys right on her heels. I closed the door after we had cleared the threshold, then watched as she put her daughter on the sofa. She began to brush the hair out of Heidi's face.

"What happened, baby? Tell momma what happened."

Heidi wasn't crying anymore, but she was catatonic, staring straight ahead. I knelt beside her and took her hand. I would have to be the one to tell Mrs. Collins what happened. I touched Heidi's mom gently on the shoulder. When she turned to look at me I jerked my head away; she stood and followed me until we were out of earshot.

"The four of us, Heidi and us guys, decided to look for little Sarah ourselves," I began. "And unfortunately... we found her."

Ariana Collins fixed her eyes on me; they were wide and frightened. "Is she okay?" Her voice was no more than a hoarse whisper, and it was touched with a bit of dread; she was even shaking her head slightly as she asked.

I shook my head firmly in return. "She's dead."

R.W.K. Clark

CHAPTER 6

The atmosphere on the 'Diamond of the Sea' cruise ship changed somewhat after Sarah Mills' remains were found. I personally was surprised that it didn't change more. I thought a little girl's life deserved the respect of mourning, even from strangers.

It seemed that some of the passengers went into a state of mourning, though. Sarah's parents, along with her remains, were picked up by helicopter, and the space she was found in was cleaned out, the rotten water removed by men with special suits and gear. Deck 3 was off limits for some time, making passengers whose staterooms were there be forced to stay inside, except to go to meals in one of the two restaurants on that deck.

Kids were no longer seen playing or running around. When one was spotted so were their parents, and they would have a tight grip on them in one way or another. The topic of conversation all over was the water in the compartment, and how it had gotten there. Rumor had it that it leaked from a large barrel, which was being transported for study when the ship docked.

Many people wanted to get off the ship and go

home. Suddenly, the waters didn't look so beautiful anymore. The reality of our tainted planet seemed to hit almost everyone in the face hard because of little Sarah's death. But the truth is, it didn't affect everyone; not the majority, in fact. Sadly, those it did affect let it go after a very short time. It seemed that soon the entire incident would be forgotten. Neither I nor any of my three friends could believe the callousness being demonstrated regarding the girl's death.

But the incident of finding her formed a bond between Heidi and me that would never be broken. The ship's doctor had treated her with sedatives and ordered her to bed rest; by the next day she was more herself, and she had come to find me first thing the next morning before my parents, and I had even left for breakfast. I had been the one to respond to her light tapping at our door, and the rush of relief I felt when I saw her gave me a warmth all over.

"Hi," she said when she saw me, a slight smile on her face. Her eyes looked puffy, tired, and sad, though. I knew she had a rough night. "Sorry about falling apart on you like that. I… I just couldn't believe it. I guess, in a way, I still can't."

My first instinct was to hug her, so I did. I knew how I felt when I saw the bones and blood; she was sure to have felt the same. I stood there in the corridor, hugging her until she loosened up and looked at me. She leaned forward and gave me a long, leisurely kiss on the lips, sending shocks up and down my spine. I kissed her back.

"Are you feeling okay, though?" I finally asked when we pulled away from each other. "You don't have to stay in bed?"

Heidi shrugged. "I'm better, and the doctor said I could get up and around as soon as I felt like it. He wants me to freely discuss my experience and feelings as soon as I am able. I'll take a raincheck on that one she laughed. I could use some company, though. Will you hang out with me?"

I turned toward the room to see my mother and father putting jackets on. "Hold on," I said, then went into our stateroom. "I'm going to skip breakfast today. Heidi needs to talk."

They didn't even answer me; my mother simply offered me a nod of understanding. Even though they were fairly staunch about us dining together, I knew they wouldn't press the issue. They respected that I had gone through something fairly traumatic. Not to mention the fact that both of them had changing feelings about the colorful, bubbling liquid holding the ship up. The reality of what it could do seemed to have them thinking. They had even skipped their photography class.

I stepped back into the corridor and gently closed the door behind me, then proceeded to put my arm protectively around her shoulders. "Where do you want to go? Have you eaten yet?"

Heidi shook her head. "I'm hungry, though. Have you?"

"No. Let's get a bite together." I thought about it

for a minute. "Let's go to American Icon. I love their French toast."

We took the elevator, which wasn't busy at all, much to our surprise. The still atmosphere was probably due to the discovery of Sarah and the manner in which she died. It seemed that many passengers were staying in that day. In fact, the restaurant was almost empty, and we managed to get a table alone, away from everyone else.

After ordering, I reached across the table and took Heidi by the hands. "So, are you holding up all right, then?"

"Yeah," she replied, looking almost embarrassed. "My parents are a mess, especially my dad. He can't believe this has happened. They called him to help last night; they wanted to figure out how the water leaked from the barrel. He told me the water had eaten right through, Tripp. It ate right through the barrel. He wants off the ship, but we can't leave because of his job. He said if it can eat through the barrel it can also eventually eat through the hull of a ship like this. I just want to go home."

Tears formed in her eyes, and a single one trickled down her cheek. Heidi absentmindedly wiped it away, embarrassment in her eyes. "I'm sorry. I just can't stand the thought that that little girl was playing a game. I keep thinking about what it was like for her, dying under there like that. Oh, yeah. My dad also said, from what he can see from the barrel's sample, the water has mutated, and it's not good."

"Even your father said it would have been quick if she fell overboard," I replied in a soothing tone. "I'm sure it was quick in that compartment, too. It's the water, Heidi, not the location of it."

She shook her head. "It's not just that; I'm afraid of it now, too. What if it did eat through the ship? We would all die, out here in the middle of the ocean, and most of the deaths would be because people wanted to go on some kind of stupid, sick sight-seeing trip. It's just so wrong."

"Listen, it hasn't eaten through a ship yet," I told her, but I couldn't help but think that, if it was mutating it could be doing anything; we knew nothing.

Our food came then, two plates of French toast, scrambled eggs, and sausage links. As a sixteen-year-old growing young man, I was usually hungry all the time, and I had been when we came. But now, as I sat there looking at my food, I felt nothing. As a matter of fact, it seemed as though my throat had closed up a bit. I picked up my fork and began toying with my eggs; when I looked up, Heidi was doing the same thing.

"We should both try to eat," I told her. "We need our strength."

It was a good idea, but it was much easier said than done. We sat there another twenty minutes, and by the time we decided to leave I had eaten two bites of my French toast and a single sausage link; Heidi had eaten a few bites of an egg before giving up. We left silently, holding hands and walking slowly.

"Do you want to do something?" she asked. "I'm up

for a distraction; anything to take my mind off all this."

We wound up strolling along Deck 4 and checking out all the shops before heading up to Deck 5 and visiting the few located there. When we were finished, we decided to head up top and relax. It was there that we ran into Drake and Mike, and I knew we were going to be discussing little Sarah Mills all over again. We looked at each other and braced ourselves for the next conversation.

As we sat down with the guys, Mike was the one to speak first.

"Hey, Heidi," he began. "Are you feeling better today?"

She nodded shyly but didn't answer, so I picked up the ball. "It's still rough, even for me. I mean, it's not every day you see something like that, you know?"

Drake nodded. "I'm just sorry for everyone who had to see it, but most of all I'm sorry for their parents. I'm pretty sure they're blaming themselves."

"My dad says they will more than likely sue the cruise line, and he says they'd win." Heidi finally joined the conversation. "My dad brought them because they were investors, and look what happened. But if it were any other passenger, they would be out for blood. That's how people are anymore; they get what they ask for, then they decide everyone owes them something when it goes wrong. Who could possibly think that it would be safe to go on a cruise in the middle of a completely toxic sea? A sea in which there is no life left at all? For all we know, a lawsuit for Sarah will spark hundreds more over dumb crap."

She was on a rant, and we let her go. None of us had the answer, and we lapsed into silence for a moment after she was finished. When I finally looked over at Heidi, I saw that her eyes were tearing up again and I felt altogether powerless and weak. I didn't know what to do, so I reached out and put my hand on her shoulder to give her a gentle squeeze; the world was definitely in a mess, all right, and she was broken-hearted over it, just as I was.

After a bit, she wiped at her eyes and asked, "Does anyone know what time it is?"

Mike glanced at his watch. "Eleven-fifteen."

Heidi smiled at me. "I promised my mother and father I would be back in time for lunch. Then, my dad has some kind of meeting with the captain about what happened. They want to discuss the fact that the water ate through the barrel. He wants my mother and me there with him, so I guess I'd better get going." Heidi leaned toward me, quickly and unexpectedly, and planted a lingering kiss on my cheek. "I'll see you later, Tripp?"

I smiled at her and nodded. "Whenever you want."

With that, Heidi left for the elevators. I watched her walk away until she was out of sight, my whole body warm and tingly, and my cheek still burning from her kiss. When I turned back to the guys, they were both smiling and giving me these stupid googly-eyed looks.

"Ooh, Tripp," Drake said in a falsetto tone. "I love you, Tripp. I want to marry you, Tripp, and have ten babies!"

Both of them cracked up, and even I was forced to smile a bit. Stupid heads. But part of being a guy was also a stupid head sometimes, even in the tragic age we are living in.

I'll admit, the razzing and laughing was probably the one reason I hadn't had a nervous breakdown myself.

CHAPTER 7

As it turned out, I didn't get to spend any quality time with Heidi for the rest of the day. I spoke to her that evening, after dinner, when she came to our stateroom and told me (my parents had resumed their sick photography fun) that she and her parents had been in the meeting with the ship's crew for most of the day, breaking only for meals. We made plans for the following day, and she gave me a long kiss goodbye, a kiss that I will probably never forget.

I went to bed, thinking of the softness of her lips and the smell of her hair. I dreamed we were running through green fields and laughing at stupid jokes. I dreamed of swimming in clear blue water with her, and the dream seemed so real. But, as we all know now, I woke to the reality of our sick planet, still on the ship, still floating in the toxic sea.

When I did wake, my parents were gone; I found a note telling me that I should feel free to enjoy breakfast as I pleased, as well as lunch. The note said they would be spending the day with the Roths, skydiving on Deck 16 at the 'RipCord,' a skydiving simulator. I felt relief; I didn't want to spend any time talking about little Sarah

Mills or the 'beautiful' water that had eaten her alive.

I took my time getting started. I knew that if Heidi wanted to see me, she would come. I also knew I was hungry, so I picked at the food on the cart that my parents had ordered. I did it while standing in my underwear, and I enjoyed the moment immensely.

Once I had 'showered' if you could call it that anymore, I decided that the first thing I would do was find Heidi and see if she had eaten since I hadn't heard from her yet. I knew she should be free that morning. I was still ravenous, having eaten next to nothing the day before and just a few bites off the cart. After we fueled up, I thought we could take a leisurely walk together, just to talk and get to know each other better. I hoped the cruise wouldn't be the last time I saw her, but I didn't have high hopes. We were both in high school, and I lived in Chicago while her family hailed from Miami Beach. Chances looked fairly bleak in my realist mind.

∞

So, I opened the stateroom door and left. The air seemed thin, so I gulped it in, to clear my mind and prepare for the day. I turned to the right to head to the elevators, and there she was, Heidi, coming toward me and looking as fresh as the morning dew—used to look. I felt the smile cover my face; she looked amazing.

"Good morning, Tripp," she greeted me.

I was grinning like a goon. "Good morning. You look like you feel a little better today."

"I do. My dad will be in meetings all day, and my

mother is going to shop, so I wondered if you were free?"

I nodded vigorously. "I was just coming to find you. Have you eaten?"

"No," she replied. "And I could really go for a replay of that French toast."

Hand in hand we headed back to the American Icon Grill. Surprisingly, there were still not many diners there, and once again we sat alone. We had a male waiter that morning, and when he came to take our order, I struck up a casual conversation.

"Not very busy again, huh?"

He shook his head, and his obligatory smile faltered. "No. A lot of passengers are eating in their rooms since that girl was found. The ship seems so quiet, doesn't it? I'll admit, it's a horrible thing. I can't imagine."

We nodded in response but didn't answer his question. We simply put in our order, thanked him, and took hands across the table in a replay of the day before. But this was much better; Heidi was much more cheerful, and I thought we would have a much more happy and relaxing day together.

"After we eat, would you like to walk with me?" I asked. "I thought we should take the time to get to know each other better, without the distractions we have had, you know?"

She squeezed my hands. "That's an amazing idea. I was thinking about you last night, wishing we had met in another place and time. Wishing that we were adults so we could travel and see each other once this bad dream is over."

I didn't tell her about my dream. It was out of reach, with the swimming and all. We needed to focus on the good things, not the bad, and that meant finding what we could do together, not what we wished we could do.

Our food came fast, and it was outstanding. I mean, I don't know if it was so good because I was starving, or if the lack of diners gave them more time to make it wonderful. All I can say is, as soon as our plates were in front of us, we tore in, enjoying the deliciousness, and washing it down with ice-cold milk. We ate together in contented silence, and when we were finished, we sat rubbing our bellies and moaning happily.

We started our walk on Deck 15, where the running track was. We could walk at our own pace and simply enjoy each other's company. We strolled holding hands, and it took me some time to realize that my palms weren't sweating. I was getting relaxed and much more confident around Heidi, and I wished our time together would never end.

She told me about Miami Beach, and about her friends. She filled me in on her classes at school: which ones she loved and which ones she simply tolerated for the sake of a diploma. It turned out she adored art and music; I wasn't much of an artist, but the music was life for me. We had a lot in common. The thing we discovered we had in common the most was our hatred for the laziness and lack of consideration for our planet that our species possessed, and we discussed it passionately, and at great lengths.

Were we so into each other that we lost track of time, and it wasn't until I heard a distant 'Oh, my!' that my attention was jerked back to reality. We both stopped dead in our tracks and began to look around for the person who had said it; the tone of their voice was stricken, to say the least.

When we turned, we noticed that the others who had been using the track were all now standing at the railings, looking over with their mouths hanging agape, and their faces filled with either sadness or disbelief.

"What the heck?" I muttered.

Heidi and I made our way to see for ourselves, but no amount of words or expressions could have prepared us for what we were to see.

I had no idea where we were in the sea, exactly, and it wasn't until later, after the cruise, when we arrived home, that I found out. But that doesn't even matter. What all of us saw that day made our location of no significance anymore.

A tiny island could be seen off the starboard side. You could see that at one time it had been lush with tree life, for some of them were still standing tall. But the majority of plant life, including the trees that were still standing, were a dark blue-black in color; the green was completely gone.

The sand that I could imagine had once made up some sort of beach did not exist. It seemed, at least from where we were standing, that the now dead trees and plants were growing straight up out of the ocean. Several birds circled the area, screaming in mourning.

But we were pretty close to the scene, and we were passing it slowly. The worst part wasn't the plants or the birds; rather, it was the floating bones of whatever animals had previously inhabited the tiny patch of earth. They drifted all around, floating as if on a massive blob of partially solid slime. Even from as high as we were I could see partial carcasses of unidentified, once-living things.

"Oh, Tripp," Heidi whispered. I wrapped my arm around her and pulled her close.

All I could hear were people; some sobbed, some gasped. I didn't hear many words or sentences, but perhaps I wasn't listening closely enough. It seemed to me at that exact moment, everyone who stood on that ship looking at that murdered island was basically shocked to silence.

What we were witnessing was literally the next phase, the truth about what the waters were doing. This was something they had not televised on the news or made the public aware of, though all of us should have known already. The water was killing all plant life, and we knew what that meant.

"All passengers, please return to your quarters. This is for your own safety. Please return to your quarters."

The voice coming over the intercom system was both insistent and frightened. The speaker and the rest of the crew hadn't expected this and therefore hadn't expected anyone would see it. Now the secret was out, the truth was known deeply by all who were watching. It was horrifying.

No one moved at first; we were all just staring. The second time the announcement came, it was louder and tinged with frustration and anger. People began to back away from the rail while others gathered the few children on deck and made their way to the stairs and elevators. I pulled back slightly on Heidi's shoulder to indicate we should go.

"Come on, Heidi. We have to go."

She continued to stare, tears running down her face, so I said her name more insistently. She jerked her head toward me, fear written all over her face, erasing her features. Her look said it all, but she spoke anyway. Her voice was trembling.

"This is how it is going to be everywhere, if they don't figure this out."

I pulled her to me and held her tight. I wanted to lie; I wanted to say that it would be okay, that they would fix it eventually, but I knew that wasn't true.

Slowly, but surely, I was able to guide her away from the railing and to the elevators, which now had a line. Finally, we gave up and took the stairs straight to Heidi's stateroom. I knew that her stateroom offered virtual balcony views, and I had a feeling the ship's crew would have taken control of them. That was where I wanted her to be because she was already in a somewhat fragile state after discovering Sarah Mills. I didn't think she needed to see or witness any more death or destruction.

Just as she reached for the door of her stateroom, it flew open. There stood Ariana, eyes wide and face tear-soaked. Heidi ran directly into her mother's arms.

"Oh, Mom!"

The woman squeezed her tightly while I stood there feeling completely ineffectual. Her mother looked at me over Heidi's shoulder, her eyes were frightened and full of questions. I didn't know what to say or do, so I took it upon myself to step inside the stateroom and close the door to give them privacy from the people passing in the corridor. I didn't want to leave Heidi.

I don't think we were there two full minutes when her father came. He was rushing, and looked extremely concerned for his family; as a matter of fact, he nearly bowled me over when he came in. I moved out of the way as quickly as possible, and my discomfort with being there grew. I would've left, but I couldn't bear the thought of leaving until I knew that Heidi would be okay.

He went right up to his wife and daughter and wrapped his arms around them both, sandwiching Heidi in the middle.

"You saw it, didn't you?" he asked. His voice was filled with a mixture of sorrow and disgust.

Both of them replied with tearful yesses. He glanced back at me over his shoulder and gently shook his head. After a moment they let each other go.

"I think we should all have a talk," her dad announced. "That would include you, son. Have a seat."

My stomach leaped. Why did he want to include me? Did he think I was some sort of bad influence on his daughter? After all, it seemed like every time she was with me she wound up sobbing and crying.

I nervously walked to the sofa in the sitting area and gingerly took a seat. My hands were trembling, so I clasped them together to hide the fact. Mr. Collins didn't seem too focused on me at first, and I took that as a good sign.

Once we were all seated, he began. "Tripp, I'm glad to get an opportunity to talk, though I'm sorry it is under these circumstances. Heidi tells me your parents are here on a joyride?"

I liked the way he put it because that was exactly what it was. Nodding, I said, "Yes. But, I'm embarrassed to say, they both work in a field that has contributed to the pollution problems. I am against it, and they both know it, sir."

"Heidi told me that as well," he replied. "Well, it doesn't matter. I didn't ask you to sit so I could lecture or judge you. The reason for our little talk is to discuss the island."

We all waited in silent expectation.

After taking a deep breath, he continued. "What you saw out there is going to become the norm. It is just the beginning. Anyone with a third-grade education knows what happens when living things don't have water. We all know what happens when there are no plants. The island is a perfect example of the perpetuation that is taking place. It is something that my colleagues and I are working furiously to stop. Unfortunately, we are not sure how.

"With that being said, you should know that the

governments of the world are working collectively, and privately, to find a solution. While we are not able to stop this right now, steps are being taken to save and maintain our lives on this planet. We can all have hope in survival, though I'm sure I don't have to tell you that not everyone will."

We remained quiet. My mind was going one hundred miles per hour. I wished my parents had been with Heidi and me when we saw what we saw. I would have taken them both by the backs of their necks and said, 'Look! Not so beautiful now, is it? There is no beauty in death!' But something inside of me knew that they wouldn't have been able to hear my words anyway. They were blinded by the bright colors and the deceptively lively bubbles which seemed to boil all around us, and all over the world.

Mr. Collins continued. "We are all stuck on this ship for the remainder of the cruise. Believe me, I have done my part in trying to sway this decision, but of course, the cruise line is concerned with termination suits and the like. We must stick this out, but we must also try and stay safe." He turned to me. "Talk to your parents; try to tell them what I have said. Try to keep them from ever coming back to the water again, Tripp."

I digested his words, repeating them over and over in my head as if I were chewing on a horrid, rotten lemon or some other vile food that I was struggling to swallow. After a moment of this, I stood and nodded at him.

"I will. I am going to find them right now." I paused

and looked at Heidi, whose red-rimmed eyes were fastened on me. "When it is okay with your mom and dad, come find me, okay?"

"I will, Tripp."

I left the room with a heavy heart and an aching head. My family's stateroom was three decks down, but I barely remember the walk, the elevator ride, or even my arrival. It seemed that the next thing I knew after leaving the Collins' stateroom was standing before the door to our stateroom, staring and wondering if my parents were inside or if they were out oohing and aahing at the once lush patch of destruction that appeared to float in the ocean.

When I opened the door, I was surprised to see them both sitting there. The television was off, and the stateroom was quiet. Both of them looked up when I walked in, and my mother spoke first.

"Did you hear?" she asked.

I snorted sarcastically. "Hear? I saw it. Did you?"

My father took a turn. "No. Tell us."

I sat down, crossed my arms over my chest, and leaned back on the sofa. "Well, there was no more sand; the trees were jutting out of the ocean, but they were wavering. They won't be standing long. It was horrible. Oh, yeah, and they were black with death. No oxygen coming from those things, you know?"

They just stared at me stupidly. "There is a gentleman on board who is working to help figure this mess with the water out. He says as soon as we dock we need to stay away from the water. He also said we should stay in until then."

My mother perked right up just then. "What? You know that on the last night they hold the Festival of Hues! I live for it!"

I wanted to vomit. Was my own mother, the woman who gave birth to me, really as stupid and shallow as to trade health and well-being for a moment of temporary awe directed at something that was killing us all? Could it be true?

Yes.

My father had zero backbone. If I expected in any way to live once this cruise was over, I was going to have to cut off all dependency on the Neanderthals who sat with me that day. My heart was broken due to their ignorance and apathy. I was disgusted to the core by those who had given me life, and I was deeply ashamed.

It took me a little while to process her stupid words. I could feel the anger and frustration building up inside me until it bubbled over like the tainted waters and trickled off the tip of my tongue. It was best not to say anything at all, but I seemed powerless.

"What is the matter with you people?"

Both of them continued to look at me as if they had absolutely no idea what I was talking about. Confusion was all over their faces, and they even looked a bit hurt. I just watched them both and waited for someone to say something… anything.

My father took the stage. "After all the trips we have brought you on, and all we have done…"

"What?" I asked incredulously. "Are you kidding?

Since the spill, these cruises have always been for the sole purpose of your own sick sideshow. What are you talking about?"

My father looked over at my mother, then back to the floor.

She decided to take the helm as best as she could. "You couldn't be more wrong, Tripp. We wanted to show you how beautiful it is, the glowing color. We wanted you to be surrounded by its beauty!"

I grew furious. "Beauty?" Now I stood up, my five-foot-eleven frame standing tall and rigid. "It is killing everything in the world, including people! How blind can you be? How selfish?"

I looked at them, blown away. They just stared at me as if they were a couple of misunderstood children who didn't get why their parent was yelling at them. They appeared to think I was speaking nonsense in a language they didn't understand.

I threw my hands in the air and stormed out of the stateroom. I wanted to cry; I wanted to scream.

But as I stormed off and made my way to the elevators, I realized that I had no idea where I was going or what I was doing. I reached the elevators just as an empty car was beginning to close, and I stuck my hand in blindly to stop it before boarding and punching the button for Deck 16.

It was then that the tears came, and I couldn't stop them.

R.W.K. Clark

CHAPTER 8

The car didn't stop at any other deck. I rode right to the top, and when I got out there were just a few people here and there, and none of them took note of the teenager who was crying like a baby. I looked to the left, then the right, and I saw Drake sitting all alone in our favorite spot. I breathed a sigh of relief, wiped my eyes, and headed over to him.

"Hey, Drake. What's happening?"

I startled him, and he jumped a bit, his head jerking around to see who I was. "Hey, Tripp." He turned back to view the horizon, which happened to be tinged a bit with purple, which was not normal for early afternoon. I pulled my eyes away from it and sat down next to him.

"I guess there are a bunch of passengers who want off bad enough to demand docking," he said thoughtfully. "My mom says some are even threatening to charter their own helicopters to come. I want to go home bad, man, but my parents said we are staying." He turned to me. "I saw the island from our balcony; I have a really bad feeling about this, dude."

I listened in silence and waited for a minute to respond. He said, "I just want to go home. I don't want to be on this ship in the middle of this sludge anymore. I want to go home to Michigan before all the trees are dead and the grass is gone. I want to lie in the park on my back and look at the stars. I want to walk with my feet on solid ground." He turned to me. "I wanna get off now, Tripp. I want to go home."

I nodded and gave him a macho pat on the back. I didn't know what to say, because I wanted to go home, too. I waited a moment, then asked, "Where's Mike?"

Drake shrugged, then replied. "He's with my parents. We had it out, and I ran up here. I'm sure he looked for me, but we were heading to get something to eat. He went with them for food, if I know Mike. Like I do. They were taking us to the Doghouse; it's our favorite. They have the best food…" His voice trailed off.

We were still again for a moment, then he continued. "Tripp?" he asked.

"Yeah?"

"If you had a plan, you know? A way off the ship. Would you take it?"

I thought about it for a minute. If it was a safe and foolproof plan, I knew I would. But not if it meant leaving my parents, even though they wanted to stay. I knew I might even take the chance then, but definitely not without Heidi and her family.

"I guess I would, depending on the circumstances."

Drake turned to me once again. "What if I had a plan? Would you come?"

I looked him over, studying his face to see if he was

serious. "Are you trying to make a plan, Drake? Because there are only a few ways one could even consider doing it, and I don't think they are survivable."

"Like what?"

Now it was my turn to shrug. "I don't know. I can think of two, really. One would be to jump in the water and try to swim, but we both know what the result of that would be. The other would be to steal a lifeboat. If you want to go so bad why don't you just get on a chopper, if they okay it?"

"We would have to be eighteen or have parental permission; a steward already told me that would be the case if it was approved." He paused. "A lifeboat, huh?"

He was really thinking about bailing. "Look, Drake. Even that would fail. Remember Sarah Mills? The water that killed her ate through a metal barrel, man. A lifeboat isn't going to last out there. We have a few more days, then we can all get off, and no one can force you to do this ever again."

"Yeah, I guess." He went still once again.

He dropped it then. I didn't want to leave him; he was depressed and quiet, and to be honest, I wasn't sure he was in his right mind. He was literally thinking about trying to come up with a way to leave the ship, and we were surrounded by flesh-melting toxins. Yes, he needed to be watched, at least in my mind.

As we sat there quietly, I thought about the day. I thought about the black, dead island, and I thought about all that island meant. I considered Heidi and her family, whose thoughts about the state of the world were so much like my own. I thought about Drake, and I thought about my own parents, who I was convinced would die out here if given the option.

I'm not sure how long we sat there just gazing at the sky. To be honest, I didn't care. I was doing more thinking and mental sorting than I had done since boarding, and considering all that I'd seen, I needed it.

All of a sudden, Heidi's voice came from behind us, just as it was starting to get dark.

"How long have you two been up here?" she asked.

We both turned to see her and Mike walking toward us. She was smiling, obviously relieved to have tracked me down. Mike was walking behind her a bit, with a look on his face that I couldn't read like he was a bit scared or something.

"I don't know," I replied. "A while. A few hours. It's been good, though."

When they reached us Mike took a deep breath. "Are you mad at me, Drake?"

Drake gave him a half-crocked grin. "Naw. I know you were hungry, or you would have been with me. Give me a break, dork."

Heidi sat down next to me and immediately gave me a kiss smack-dab on the lips. I blushed immediately while my two pals made goofy noises. She stuck her tongue out at them.

"I feel better," she said. "My dad says we have to stay on board for the rest of the cruise because it is for the health and welfare of the people, but he promised me I never have to come with him again."

I gave her a tight squeeze. "I'm glad. I know that I never am, and from the way it sounds, Drake agrees. Mike, how about you?"

"I only came to hang with Drake, so I'm pretty sure I can pass."

We all felt relief, and for the first time in days, I believed I might make it until docking without any real crisis to myself or those I loved. My heart felt ten pounds lighter, as did my friends'. In minutes we were joking and laughing like we had before finding Sarah, and before seeing the black, dead island and floating bones.

It was dark, and we were all heading to the elevators to return to our staterooms, when Drake said, "Hey, listen, guys. How about if the four of us hit Chops' Grille for lunch tomorrow? Say, right at noon?"

We all exchanged glances. "I'll be there!" I said, and that was followed by avid agreements by the other two.

"Awesome. So, see you two there at noon," Drake continued. "Mike and I will get the seats, so look for us inside."

They went their way, and we went ours. We didn't go right to Heidi's stateroom. Instead, we found a couple of deck chairs and hung out for a bit longer, then spent a number of minutes making out. I can honestly say that, to this point, it was the best night of my life.

∞

Tucked safely in my bed, later on, I reviewed the memory of the day in my mind. I thought of Drake and his depressed state of mind. I thought of Heidi and her parents, and how they had their heads on straight regarding all of this disaster. I thought of my own mom and dad, and my heart wept. Finally, I fell asleep, and I dreamed I was on a rotten, dripping black island, with no food or water, and no life. I tried to run and find a beach, but my legs kept sinking into the murky, poisonous sludge.

In my dream, I was dying, and I knew it.

CHAPTER 9

I woke with a start to my alarm beeping obnoxiously. I slapped at it with my hand and gave it a squinty stare: nine in the morning. I had let myself sleep in, leaving a note for my parents to leave me be. They had, obviously.

The first thing I did was jump in the shower, and I let the fake water fall over my body, ignoring the slight chemical smell which was its trademark. I cleaned up as quickly as I could, anxious to jump out from under the stream and dry it off of me. I don't think I was out five seconds when I heard a knock at the stateroom door. I stuck my head out, heard it again, and yelled, "Hold on!"

Donning a bathrobe, my hair still dripping, I cracked the stateroom door just enough to peek out. It was Heidi, looking fresh and energetic.

"Hey, sleepyhead," she grinned. "Good morning."

I pulled the robe around me tighter and stepped back, holding the door open for her. "Come on in," I muttered, embarrassed. "Give me a minute; I need to dress."

She chuckled and sat down on the couch, picking up

the remote to the television. I stood there watching her and smiling. After a brief moment, she turned around and said, "Well, are you going to gawk at me all day, or are you going to get dressed?"

I didn't even respond. Turning on my heel, I immediately rushed to my room to dress. It seemed I would get to spend the morning with my crush, and I was very pleased.

This time we had breakfast at The Café on Deck 5. We enjoyed it light that morning: yogurt, fresh fruit, and juice and milk. Heidi and I flirted and teased. Our conversation was mostly about me and what I planned to do when I got back to Chicago. I also noticed that both of us avoided all negative or painful topics; we were ready to put the past week behind us.

We decided we would limit our walk to that deck as well. We would visit a photo gallery there, a couple of small specialty shops, and take a stroll. Since Chops' Grille, where we were meeting Drake and Mike, was on the same deck, we were pleased with our planning.

I would have to say that our stroll on the deck was the highlight of my day. At one point Heidi even pulled me, giggling, into a small, closet-like space, where we kissed until my knees turned weak. I don't know how long we were in there, but I was fearful I was in need of a serious cold shower by the time we were ready to head to Chops'. She laughed at me while I waited for 'normalcy' to return to my lower region.

By five to twelve we were approaching Chops', giggling and laughing, both enamored with each other. I smiled and waved to a steward standing at his post talking to a woman and pointing toward the other end of the deck. He waved back.

"He's a short dude, isn't he?" I asked Heidi.

She looked at the man, who had turned his full attention back to the female passenger. "Yeah, he is. What do you think, about five foot four?"

"That's about right," I replied. "I've never had that problem. How tall are you?"

"Five-two, but I'm a girl," she said with a smile.

Inside Chops' we were seated quickly. Drake and Mike were there, as promised. He had taken the liberty of ordering four big steaks. When I tried to resist, he informed me it was too late; besides, he wanted to treat us, and we should let him, he said.

I would have to say that lunch was the first time I really sat down with my two pals and listened about their lives. Mike talked more than he had since I had met him. Drake seemed a little off, I have to admit, especially looking back on it now. But at the time I thought he was still upset over the island. I even remember telling myself not to worry, that he would be better once he was off the ship.

For dessert, we had cherry cheesecake all around. It was wonderful, and by the time we were done I was so full, I couldn't move. We sat there digesting and talking idly about nothing and everything.

Right before we left, Drake said, "You know, Tripp, when you get home from this cruise you should look me up. We can get together and laugh about how we survived this nightmare."

"I'd like that," I replied.

He reached into the breast pocket of his button-down and withdrew a small piece of paper. "Here's my number; get ahold of me when this is all over, okay?"

"I'll do that."

The series of events that happened next—even to this day they remain a bit fuzzy. Bits and pieces are a blur, yet it seems I remember all of it clearly at the same time. It happened fast, faster than anything I can recall in my life, even now, that it was all in slow motion.

We were walking out of Chops' Grille, the four of us. Heidi was telling us about some girl she went to grade school with, and how the girl used to pick on her. It was a funny story, and we were chuckling as she told it. I remember seeing the steward standing at his post to my right; he was laughing at something a passenger was saying to him, and then, as we walked, I recall the passenger playfully slapping him on the shoulder and walking away.

Just as we were getting ready to pass him, Drake brushed against me hard. In my mind, I thought he just wanted to walk on the other side of me, but within seconds of his brushing I heard a loud holler, and it came from within inches from me, or so it seemed. I turned to see who it was, and I saw Drake had the steward in a headlock with a steak knife to the man's throat. People began to scream.

"Drake, what the heck?" I yelled. "What are you doing?"

His eyes were wide and crazy. The hand which held the knife to the steward's throat was shaking like mad. Passengers all around us were either hiding behind stuff or screaming their brains out. I felt like I was in a dream, and I didn't know what to do.

"It's okay, Tripp," he hollered back. "I have a plan! This guy is going to help me lower a lifeboat. I'm getting off this ship today!"

"Wh-what?" the steward stammered.

Drake put his lips to the man's ear. "I said, you are going to get in that lifeboat over there with me, and you are going to lower it, and we are getting off this boat together. I'm going home."

The steward's eyes darted around at the crowd that was quickly gathering. "It's okay, people. Stay calm!" he yelled.

"Drake, you need to rethink this," I said. I was holding my hand out to him. "Just give me the knife; we'll go to your stateroom, and your mom and dad can calm you down a bit."

"They don't care about how I feel, or about the fact that we are all gonna die out here!" He was out of his mind, and I thought to myself that I should have seen this coming.

Heidi spoke up. "Drake, we're docking in a few days. You can make it until then!"

"Docking in a few days!" He screamed as his eyes darted crazily. He began to back up, dragging the petrified steward with him. "I'm off this ship today, Heidi! Today!"

He continued to back up toward the closest lifeboat. I heard people running, and I turned to see a group of crew persons heading toward us, one being the ship's captain. When he reached us, he stopped and held both of his hands out in front of him.

"Listen, we can talk about this and work something out to get you off the ship," he said. "Just let him go before both of you get hurt."

Drake shook his head. "There is no working anything out with you people. I can't even take a helicopter! No one will get hurt if you just give me a lifeboat and lower it!"

The captain kept his hands up. "Okay, okay. Listen, what's your name, son?"

"Stop!" Drake replied as he continued to back up.

I said to the captain, "His name is Drake Nelson."

"Okay, Drake. Let's just slow down." The captain kept his eyes fastened on the knife in Drake's hand. "We'll get you a lifeboat."

He turned to one of his crew members and said something I couldn't hear. The guy ran off, and the captain proceeded to tell two others to prepare a lifeboat, which they immediately set about doing. Drake backed into a corner, so the two of them weren't behind him; he wasn't letting anyone out of his sight.

It didn't take them long to prepare the lifeboat. Just as Drake got on it with his hostage, who had gone completely pale and looked as if he might be sick, his parents came running up, followed by the crew member who the captain had sent off. Both of his parents looked extremely stricken with concern.

"Drake Joseph, you stop this now!" his mother screamed. "This cruise will be over in a week; look when we stop in Mexico we will get off. You don't ever have to do this again if you don't want! We can fly home."

He laughed loudly at them, and I remember that, to me, he sounded as if something had snapped in his mind. "You're right," he yelled. "But for me, this cruise is over today! Lower this now!"

He was holding the knife to the guy's throat so tightly that I could see it was scraping his skin with little dots from the serrated blade. "Drake, you're hurting him, man!"

My stomach was doing flips. The captain ordered that the lifeboat is lowered, and it slowly started down. I ran for the railing, along with everyone else, and we watched as it hit the vile water below. The impact surprised Drake, and he stumbled. Right then, it seemed his hostage found his courage; he turned around and tried to push Drake away from him, but he wasn't strong enough. Drake stumbled slightly, then went at the man as if he were trying to tackle him.

That was when they both went over the side and right into the water.

Everyone screamed all at the same time, including me. I watched, in horror, as someone died in the bad water for the first time before my very eyes. It seemed that they both flailed for a moment, as though they were going to try to swim away. The horrid thing was, there was no actual splashing; the water seemed to appear almost solid, shifting beneath them.

In seconds they both stopped moving completely, and I could literally see what appeared to be their clothes melting.

Mrs. Nelson was crying and screaming hysterically. Mr. Nelson was holding her to keep her from jumping over the side to her son, who was obviously already dead. I was standing there, stunned, holding Heidi, who was crying on my shoulder and could barely stand. I turned to see Mike sitting cross-legged on the deck, his eyes staring straight ahead at nothing.

I heard the captain say, "We need to clear the deck immediately."

I didn't know what to do. I didn't know if I should stay or go if I should try to comfort the Nelsons or scream with fear and anger. All of this could have, should have, been avoided. No one should have been out on that cruise ship. People were dying left and right.

"We have to go, Heidi."

We began to back away from the scene slowly, and when we were a fair distance, we both turned and ran. We got near the restrooms, and Heidi stopped dead in her tracks and vomited all over the deck. I just let her; after all, I wanted to puke too.

When she was done, she sat back hard on her butt and scooted away from her mess. With her back leaning against a wall she drew her knees up and rested her arms there, with her head down. I sat down next to her and put my arm around her, and we sat like that in silence for several minutes.

"I don't think I can take any more of this, Tripp," she finally muttered.

I didn't respond, because I felt the same way, and I didn't think there were any words of comfort. We were trapped for the time being, like inmates in a penitentiary. Tears began to stream silently down my face.

Just like we had all been saying to each other: I was more than ready to end this trip.

R.W.K. Clark

CHAPTER 10

When we docked in Mexico, it was amazing how many passengers didn't re-board, but it was in no way surprising. Heidi's father wanted his wife and daughter to fly home from there as well, but they refused to leave him. To be honest, as selfish as this sounds, I was relieved. I knew, deep in my heart, that the chances of Heidi and me never seeing one another again was high. When she told me that they would finish out the cruise, it was difficult not to show my secret delight.

My parents and I went on land, ate, and did some shopping. Because of the emergencies which had recently taken place, the ship's captain decided that we wouldn't set out again until after breakfast; we had to be back on board by ten in the morning. We ended up getting a hotel for the night; we could have returned to our stateroom, but I literally begged my parents for a break. They weren't about to cut their fun time short, so they compromised. We ended up getting a suite at the Grand Park Royal, and I isolated myself in my room from the time we got there until it was time to leave, only eating breakfast with my parents when it was ordered.

When it was time to board, the number of passengers who had 'bailed out' was embarrassingly obvious. Compared to the stampede that left the ship, the number lining up to return was nothing more than a trickle. Sure, some had stayed on board for the night, but even when we got back on one could easily tell by the people who were here that the ship lost at least half of its load of passengers.

We set out, and some announcements were made over the intercom system. First, condolences for the families and loved ones of those who had fallen victim to the waters during the outing. Secondly, the captain found it very important to explain that the Environmental Protection Agency, the Food and Drug Administration, and the Department of Natural Resources, along with other agencies from affected countries, were working together to investigate the demolished island we saw. They were also working to determine how much of the mainland was being affected, and what could be done to stop, or at least slow the process.

Next, he gave abundant 'thank yous' to those who decided to stay on board and finish out the cruise. He played up the big 'Festival of Hues,' the big to-do they held with lights and fireworks on the final night before docking for good. He used words like 'tradition,' 'loyalty,' and 'celebration of man.' It was nothing more than sugar-coated baloney.

Finally, he announced that they were planning a large, ballroom-style dance for all ages, featuring a buffet of the finest foods and beverages. The remaining days left at sea he promised to make them the best in the history of the 'Diamond of the Sea.' Then he bid us best wishes, and said, "Enjoy the remainder of your vacation."

The first thing I did when I got back to my stateroom was throw my things on my bed and prepare to find out if Heidi had re-boarded. I was scared to find out; at that point, I was sure her father had insisted. I wanted nothing more than to see her; I wanted to take her to the dance with me. I wanted to do everything with her there was to do on that vessel. I hoped and prayed it wasn't too late.

"Tripp, your father, saw the Roths when we got back on," my mother said to me as I got ready to leave. "You haven't been eating with us; we wondered if you wanted to have lunch with all of us?"

I stopped with my hand on the knob of the door, and I didn't turn around to face her. "I'm planning to find Heidi, and if she's still here, I also plan to spend as much of my time with her as her parents will allow. So, um, probably not."

I felt her hand on my arm. "Can we talk, Tripp? I mean, since Dad's not here?"

I turned around without looking at her and sat down on the sofa. "What's up, Mom?"

My mother sat; she knew it would put me off if she tried to hug or touch me too much. "Well," she began, "I just want you to know that I did quite a bit of thinking last night. Um... I think I'm beginning to see things your way."

I looked up at her. "What do you mean?"

"Well," she said slowly as she fidgeted with her wedding ring, "I started to consider everything. You know, the little girl, the dead island. But most of all I thought about your friend, Drake. I couldn't get him out of my mind all night, and I had to ask myself, 'How bad are things really, if a teenage boy, who was happy and well-adjusted, took a hostage and tried to escape a cruise?' "

I didn't answer or offer up any response. I wanted her to process all of this on her own. I wanted her to see the reality for what it really was. I noticed she had tears in her eyes, and I didn't say anything; the tears and pain were part of the reality. She plucked a tissue from a fancy silver dispenser on the end table and dabbed at her eyes, then continued.

"The thing with Drake made me think about when I was your age. Suddenly, for the first time in a long time, I thought about what the world was like then; you know, nature and all." She stopped and blew her nose, then grabbed another tissue; the tears were starting to fall now. "Remember dolphins? And whales? Now we see computer-generated sea life. I've become so preoccupied with my sick perspectives that I'd forgotten."

"I remember," I replied in a low, sad voice. "I hope I never forget."

She looked me in the eye for the first time. "I see now that taking these trips, participating in the photography and festivals, it all supports the sick outlook, you know? As long as a buck can be made they will drag their heels trying to fix it. I've contributed to this, Tripp, each and every year since the spills."

She was picking her tissue apart nervously now; bits of it fell to her lap in tiny fluffs, mussing her outfit. "I'm sorry, Tripp. I want you to know I won't be playing a part in this ever again. Your father doesn't want to leave because getting a refund will ultimately cost us more time and money, and our company would likely frown on it. Oh, I'm quitting my job, by the way, and I have adamantly encouraged him to consider doing the same. We need to be part of the solution instead of the problem. I think our talents would be better used somewhere else."

I couldn't sit there anymore. I stood and walked to my mother and then fell to my knees. I took her into my arms and held her tight. My mother cried in my arms for the first time in my life. It hurt terribly, but I felt so proud. The tears were those of someone with remorse, and my heart swelled with love.

Now, I couldn't tell you how long we sat like that, but it was a while. I didn't pull away; I wanted her to know she had my support, no matter the cost. So, I held her and let her cry for some time. Suddenly, there was a light knock on the door, and she abruptly pulled away.

"Would you get that, dear?" she asked as she stood. "I need to wash my face and fix my makeup."

Mom rushed off to the bathroom, and I went to answer the door. When I opened it my heart nearly exploded—Heidi. She looked beautiful and refreshed.

"Heidi, you're here!"

We caught each other up in a hug, and I kissed her hair over and over again. At last, I stood back, my hands on her shoulders. I couldn't believe she had gotten back on board.

"Yeah, well, my dad tried to insist that we go home, but neither my mother nor I would do that." She shrugged. "He needs our support. He's in a tough spot, too."

I couldn't stop smiling. "I'd be lying if I said I wasn't happy."

"Me, too."

I closed the door to the stateroom. "Do you want to walk? I want to do all I can with you before this is over. We can hit every activity, every event. We can go to the dance together, and the festival. Oh, and wait until you hear about my mom."

We started up the corridor, hand in hand. "Well," she replied, "we have a few days left. We can fit in quite a bit. So, what about your mom?"

For the next hour or so, we walked and talked. I filled her in on my mother's change of heart. We discussed how my mother was even going to quit her job. I could tell she was pleased for me, and it made me feel good to know someone really got me, someone really cared.

I stopped walking at one point. I turned to her and took her by the hands. I felt like if I didn't tell her what was on my mind, I never would, and I would regret it for the rest of my life.

"Heidi," I began nervously. "I've never had a girlfriend; I'm sort of the 'studious' type in life, you know? But I... I... I love you. And even if we never see each other again, at least I told you. You don't have to say it back; I don't expect that. I just had to tell you."

She smiled shyly, and a blush rose to her cheeks. "I love you too, Tripp."

I think I let out the biggest sigh of relief of my life. I started to laugh, and so did she. We started walking again, this time too busy grinning to talk. After about five minutes of peaceful, happy silence she finally spoke up.

"So, do you wanna go have lunch at American Icon?" she asked. "We can get a map of the ship and plan the perfect days together. It will be like we are on vacation together, you and me."

I turned to her and grinned; she was the female version of me, and I was head over heels. "Let's do it."

R.W.K. Clark

CHAPTER 11

From that moment on, it was the beginning of the best cruise I had ever been on in my life, and I had been on many.

For one thing, the atmosphere on the boat changed dramatically. With most of the stressed and mourning and frightened gone, it was less crowded and far less emotional. Every now and then you would overhear someone discussing Sarah Mills, or Drake and the steward, or the 'politics' of the dying planet, but mostly there was a strong sense that all of it was behind us, at least for now.

We ate burgers and fries at the Icon, and we planned the rest of our cruise together. It was a beautiful day, so we decided to begin things right away. We would begin on the very top—Deck 16. We would go up in the NorthStar, visit the SeaPlex, and then do a bit of gaming next door. If we chose to, which I hoped we did, we would even skydive at RipCord. Neither of us really wanted to do the surfing simulator; it was just too bittersweet.

After returning to our staterooms to tell our parents our plans, we headed out. I had a camera in hand; there was absolutely no way I would miss getting as many pictures of my beautiful companion as I could. They would be all I had to remember someday, and I cherished the opportunity more than words could say.

According to our guide, the line for NorthStar, which is basically a ride that takes you high up and gives you amazing views and photo ops, was on Deck 15. But when we arrived there was hardly anyone waiting; I had anticipated a long line, but no. There were a handful on the ride, and we were able to get some great shots of the horizon and speak to each other without hollering. It was more than I expected, or even hoped for. We even kissed while we were up there, and got a selfie of it with the view in the background. The colors of the poisoned ocean could be clearly seen, but we didn't care; it was all about us. Unforgettable!

SeaPlex didn't take up any time; it was all television screens with computer images, and it wasn't conducive to the 'moving on' we were attempting to do. We managed to get some gaming in, and we had time to skydive at RipCord before having dinner at the Kung Fu Chopsticks restaurant.

After all of that, we returned to our staterooms to shower and change. My father sat in silence in the sitting area; he was all alone, and he didn't have the television on for a change.

"Where's Mom?" I asked, looking around the dim room.

He sighed. "She's with Mrs. Roth at the fitness center."

"Oh." I started to head to my room, but thought better of it and stopped. "Are you okay, Pops?"

My dad gave a weak chuckle. "Yeah, I guess. I mean, it seems I have reached one of those points in my life where… well, I'm at a crossroad, I guess."

"Wanna talk about it?"

He shook his head. "No. I just need to face facts and act accordingly. I'll be fine, son."

I didn't know what to say. I felt bad, because his sadness, or grief, or whatever it was, was tangible. But my father wasn't much of a gabber. He dealt with things better on his own. I showered and put on some of my best clothes. Heidi and I were going to go party at the teen disco. I was excited because I had never done anything like that in my life. I had never been the social butterfly, but I knew I was going to have a good time. I'd enjoy yanking splinters out of my eyes if she was with me.

When I got ready to leave, I noticed my dad was gone. I let myself worry for a moment. But, I had to pick up Heidi at her stateroom, like a real date. Before I did that, I wanted to get her a flower; I didn't want to waste any time.

I was able to get her a single rose at a tiny florist place on Deck 3, then quickly made my way to pick her up. When she opened the door she took my breath away: her long, dark red hair was swept up off her neck, with little wisps hanging down all around. She wore a dark green silk dress that left her shoulders bare. I could hardly breathe.

"I'm going to consider this my prom," I told her after we kissed. "I wouldn't want to go with anyone else, you know."

She smiled. "Me, too. So, are you ready to dance the night away?"

After tending to the rose, I offered her my elbow, and she gracefully slid her little arm through it.

"My lady?"

"My dear!"

I was nervous, but it was foolish to be. We had more fun that evening than I ever had in my life. I wasn't much of a dancer, and to be honest, neither was she. But together we were corny magic and silly dreams. Even though there were other kids there, many who were far better dancers than we, it was as though we were all alone. We were the happiest in the world.

By the time we left, we were messy and sweaty. We went to Deck 16 to walk and watch the stars, but we wound up dancing and twirling most of the time. After a long while, we reclined on deck chairs and told each other stupid jokes and laughed.

I didn't want it to end.

We got to her stateroom around twelve-thirty. She was carrying her shoes, and my tie hung loosely around my neck. For the longest time, we stood there, just looking into each other's eyes and grinning like dummies.

"So, breakfast tomorrow?" she asked, breaking the wonderful silence.

"Yeah. French toast."

Heidi stood on her tiptoes and put her arms around my neck, her little high-heels dangling from her hands behind my back. At first, she just looked deep in my eyes and smiled, but soon the smile faded. Before I knew it, her lips were on mine, and her tongue was poking in my mouth.

We kissed for a long time. Suddenly, she pulled away and quickly said, "I'll see you in the morning, my dear."

Then she was gone.

I was shaking like a leaf. I stared at her stateroom door forever before finally forcing myself to walk away. I whistled all the way back to my quarters.

I can honestly say it was one of the best nights of my life.

R.W.K. Clark

CHAPTER 12

The plans we made were thorough, and the day ahead was packed full of things we would do together, memories we would make. First, we would have breakfast, so I rose early to dress and spend a bit of time with my parents before heading out for the day. I wanted them to know I loved them.

When I left my room both of them were sitting at the small dining table in their robes. They looked up at me from their steaming cups of coffee and smiled. It was nice to see them happy.

"Seeing your friend?" my father asked.

I nodded. "All day. Are you two set?"

My mother took a breath, set her coffee down, and sat back. "Yeah. We're going to be spending most of the time until we dock right where we are. It's time to pay attention to each other."

I hesitated. "Do you want me to stay?"

She shook her head. "Absolutely not! The rest of the trip is yours. We will, how should I say, entertain each other." I saw a twinkle in her eye, and when I glanced at my father he was staring down at his coffee, his face beet-red.

"I see," I told them. "Well, you two kids stay out of trouble, you hear?"

I headed for the door, and my dad's voice stopped me. "What are you two going to do?"

I turned and smiled at him, offering him a wink. "Everything we can."

I left my parents in the stateroom with a smile on my face.

∞

"Okay, Tripp. First on the list: five laps walking around the track, then rock climbing!"

We had just left Icon, and we were satisfied and happy. Five leisurely laps would be a perfect forerunner to hitting the rock climbing wall on Deck 15. I, personally, had been rock climbing several times, but it was a first for my cute little companion, and she could hardly wait.

We didn't go to the track for laps with exercise on our minds. Of course, the walking would help the food in our stomachs to settle before we hit the rock wall, but mostly we wanted the time to walk and talk, getting to know each other better and better. We had talked about the future of the world many times, and both of us knew it didn't look good. We agreed adamantly, even making a pact, that we would find each other when we had cars and were old enough, but like I said, we were both keenly aware of the state of our reality.

The obvious could easily be true: we might never see each other again after the boat docked for good. It was important to both of us, being first-time love birds swept off our feet, that if we wanted to know each other, enjoy each other, and have lifelong memories, it was up to us, right here and right now. So, parents put aside, we selfishly kept our time to ourselves.

I'm sure that when we walked on the track, we got on the nerves of a couple of avid joggers; they were forced to go around us, and we were holding hands. There were some runners, who would groan or flash nasty looks at us with each and every lap they did. It was a bit entertaining, I might add, and when they would get out of earshot, we would laugh at their selfish impatience and make jokes. But in all reality, we talked about what a shame it was that they were using their time like that, to grouch and complain, rather than spending it with their significant others or family. If that cruise taught us anything, it was that life could end at any minute, quickly and quietly; hadn't they learned that, too?

We wound up losing count of our laps anyway. Heidi told me stories of her life at home, tales of her grandparents, and even of a younger brother who had died at four when a ball had rolled into their street, and he had run out to retrieve it. He had been struck hard enough by a drunk driver to knock him out of his little shoes, and he had died immediately. The driver had kept going for two blocks at high speed before crashing into a telephone pole at the end of a dead-end street. The driver walked away, facing criminal charges, of course. Heidi and her parents would never be able to walk away, and they would never see or hold their little Henry Jack again.

It had been ten in the morning, in the 'safety' of their gated community.

She didn't shed a tear when she told me, though she had witnessed it and recalled the incident in great detail. When I asked her why she didn't cry she told me she had been six, and with time the sting, if not the memory, had faded. She also shared that she realized how much of a waste of time it was to cling to the dead; death was beyond our control, and life went on. It was best for those left behind to grieve and heal, but let go and cling to the good stuff. I admired her intelligence, strength, and wisdom, and I wondered if I would ever meet another girl like her again.

The rock wall was pleasantly un-crowded. A gentleman who appeared to be in his forties was halfway up the tougher section, while a boy about my age was trying his footing on the more intermediate challenges. Since Heidi was a newbie, I planned to use the easier one anyway. It didn't take long for her to master it, though, and she was ready to move up to a better challenge; before long she wanted to race, and she ended up kicking my butt.

We left the area and lounged in a couple of deck chairs before going to get lunch. We both just breathed and caught our breath for a while; I was dreaming of ice water and tacos. I glanced over at her to find her smiling at me.

"What?" I asked.

She shrugged. "Are you pissed because I beat you?"

I laughed out loud. "No way. I let you win."

"Haha!"

I could feel myself blushing. "Okay, okay. Beginner's luck."

She sat up and turned to me fully, crinkling her nose at me as she grinned impishly. The tiny sprinkling of freckles on it gave me goosebumps; she was so cute I could hardly stand it. Maybe I had subconsciously let her win; I could hardly think when I was around her.

"Fine, mister," she retorted. "It's your story, so you tell it like you want to."

She grabbed my hand and pulled me to my feet. "Let's eat. I'm hungry, and it's nearly noon. Where to?"

"How about tacos?" I suggested. "Any way we want them: unhealthy, quick, and delicious!"

Not to mention Taco Stop was right there on that deck, and my stomach was talking to me. I started to stretch when she punched me in the arm. I jumped and rubbed the sore spot, looking at her with surprise.

Another impish grin. "Tag! You're it!"

She took off like a shot, leaving me to stand there stupidly. After a second I took off on her heels, and we laughed as we ran. A steward ended up stopping us, scolding us, and telling us, 'No running!' We gave him 'yes sirs' before taking off again, our laughter echoing in his ears.

He mumbled just loud enough for us to hear, "Damn kids…"

R.W.K. Clark

CHAPTER 13

After lunch, we planned to see a movie on Deck 14, but it wasn't scheduled to begin until almost two-thirty. We decided to both shower and change, then meet up in the lounging area on Deck 14 called 'The Living Room.' There were furnishings meant for relaxation, and it would be a great place to kick back and relax.

In the elevator, on the way to her deck, Heidi said, "I think we should plan for you and me to eat together with all our parents. What do you think?"

The suggestion took me back. I hadn't even thought about us getting together with the parents, and I was a bit embarrassed. Now, though, I had nothing to hide; my parents seemed to be coming out of their insane mindset.

"You know, if we do that we may have a better chance of seeing each other when this is over," I replied. "Good idea, but I want to see how my folks are. You know, if their attitude is the same, or if they are 'reverting.' I don't want arguments between mine and yours, because that could do more damage than good."

"Talk to them," she said as we stepped off the elevator and onto the deck and started for her stateroom. "I'll do the same. I think it would be good, you know… for the future."

At her door, she gave me a long kiss, and we hugged as if we weren't meeting up in an hour. After we finally peeled each other apart I hurried for the elevator; I needed to meet her at one-thirty in The Living Room. I had to get moving.

My parents were napping when I got back, so I jumped in the shower and got busy right away. I thought about the movie we were going to see; it was some science fiction thing, but it had a love story to it, and so I was a bit apprehensive. I knew she would be able to talk me into watching a two-hour documentary on snails if she wanted to, so I pushed it out of my mind. Besides, she wasn't the kind of girl to go for straight mush, so I was probably safe.

After I had dressed, I walked out of my room to see my parents awake and dressed.

"Hi, Tripp," Dad said. "How was the morning?"

"Great!" I replied, grinning from ear to ear. "We had tacos."

My mother was looking at me and smiling. "Jim, our boy is smitten."

"I see that." They were obviously amused. "When will we get to spend a little time with this girl? Anyone who has caught your eye has to be worth knowing."

I took a breath and sat down, giving the clock a glance. I had time to take a minute. "Speaking of which, Heidi would like for you two and her parents to get together with us for dinner before we dock one night.

What do you think?"

They looked at each other briefly, then Mom said, "We would love to. As a matter of fact, we are very interested in what we could learn about all of this from her dad. You told us he was working on the pollution; that was his job, right?"

I nodded.

"Well, then," she continued, "since we are 'changing our ways,' so to speak, then yes. Let us know what night; we have no plans for the rest of the cruise."

I stood, smiling like a fool. "Awesome. That's just great. I have to meet her now, so I'll get a time and let you know."

I left, beaming like I had swallowed the sun. My heart felt a little lighter because I agreed that we had a better chance of continuing our relationship if our parents met and actually got along. Maybe they would even become die-hard disciples of the truth by learning it from Mr. Collins.

I enjoyed the feeling without hesitation or doubt. I could hardly wait to set a time for dinner with our parents and do the deal. But for now, I had a date with Heidi, and she would be happy to hear what I had to say.

My girl was waiting for me outside of The Living Room. She was wearing a bright yellow sundress with tinges of orange around the hems. The orange gave the impression that her clothes were being licked by flames, and the color set off her hair and eyes like no other.

"You look chipper," she said as I approached her.

"Ask me why." I took her hand, and we went in to find some loungers. A long one with two pillowed ends was available, so we took it right away, lying back and getting comfortable.

"Why?" she asked when we were settled.

I put my hands on her shoulders so I could see her eyes better. "My parents want to have dinner with us. They are even anxious to learn what your dad knows. They also want to get to know you. The future is so bright we need sunglasses, Heidi."

"Awesome!" she replied, propping herself up on her elbows. "How about Saturday evening? It was my dad's suggestion."

I nodded and closed my eyes. "Perfect!"

After a bit, she asked, "How did your parents get so blindsided by the spills?"

I didn't even have to think about it. "The money."

"What do you mean?"

I thought about it for a moment. "Well, they work, or I can now say 'worked,' for the company that developed the spilled chemical. When it happened, my mom defended the company and the chemical that my father helped create. In the process, in order to win the battles they faced, they had to cause people to focus on the appeal, so they 'sold' the spill, so to speak, and a lot of that was my mother's doing. Anyway, the money started pouring in, and I guess it blinded them both. But I think they were blind before that, anyway. That's the gist of it, though."

"Corporate America in all its glory," she replied in a

distracted voice.

That statement said it all. The world was being led to the slaughter like sheep, as were those doing the leading. The almighty dollar was an influential demon indeed.

"So, what do you want to study in college?" she asked. "I mean, what do you want to do?"

I didn't have to think about the answer. "I was thinking hard about getting into the clean-up and improvement aspect of all this, but after this cruise…" I paused for a bit. "Now I am seriously considering teaching."

"What would you teach?"

"Something related to the care of the environment and planet," I said. "I'm not sure, but I'll figure it out as I go. I just think an ounce of prevention is truly worth a pound of cure, and prevention starts with knowledge, you know?"

"Yeah."

"How about you?" I sat up all the way, cross-legged and leaning forward. "What are you going to do?"

She emulated my movements. "My dad would love for me to follow in his footsteps, but I'm going to work with kids somehow. Kids with either special needs, or kids who are in the system, like abused and neglected. I just want to work with kids, I don't really care how."

"That's a good one," I said. "It helps build the future."

She smiled at me, and I could see the love clearly in her eyes. I wondered if she could see it in mine. Slowly, Heidi leaned forward, and I didn't hesitate to meet her halfway. We kissed, and I melted right where I sat. I don't know when we stopped; I just sat there with my eyes closed and a goofy smile on my face.

Suddenly, she said, "Are you ready?"

My eyes flew open. "For what?"

Heidi broke out in lilting laughter. "For the movie, goon. It starts in ten minutes."

Ten minutes? Where had the time gone? I could have sworn we had been there for ten minutes ourselves! I let out a long sigh and stood, offering my hand to help her up.

I wished that stopping the clock was something human beings could do.

∞

The movie was called 'Fever Ground.' It was about the world nearing the sun slowly but surely. As the days passed, the temperatures rose, and the people of Earth were literally cooking to death.

The main characters were a young, twenty-something couple, and the storyline chronicled the days before the end of the world. Power went out, the water dried up, and the population panicked. Robberies and murders were rampant, and this pair of lovebirds raced to find a safe haven from destruction.

But there was none.

There was no happy ending, either. Yes, it was a love story, and there were lots of parts that were romantic and sentimental. But mostly it was scary and sad, and I can speak for both of us when I say we left the theater deep in thought, with heavy hearts.

We walked in silence, hand in hand, processing for a short time. Heidi finally said, "You know, I can't believe they are playing that film right now. You know, with the water and all."

I agreed. "Right? But did you notice, there were only four other people in there with us; it was deserted. Not a big hit with the passenger masses, I take it?"

"Probably makes them face too much reality." She glanced at her watch. "It's almost five; hungry?"

"Let's eat light," I suggested. "My stomach is a bit bent out of shape after two hours of that."

So, we had chef salads at the Icon. I had suggested trying another place, but my heart hadn't been in it. I just offered for her sake. She quickly shot me down, however. It turned out my love interest was as much a creature of habit as I.

We planned to spend the evening at the H2O Zone, which was pretty much a small, onboard water park, but now it didn't use water. I didn't like using the 'fake' water much, and usually limited myself to showers; no swimming. I was planning to compromise, but when we were leaving, and I mentioned our changing into our swimsuits, Heidi tensed up.

"Look," she began, "Let's not dip in the AquaSim; I never do it if I can help it. How do you feel about going to the library, getting a book, and taking it to Café Two70. We could read together for a couple of hours. Then, we could have a yummy dessert before bed. What do you think?"

I was stunned and immensely pleased at her

suggestion. I loved to read books, even in the digital age we were stuck in. "Amazing idea. But I get to pick your book, and you get to pick mine."

"I love it!" she exclaimed. "Let's go!"

We decided we would read for two hours at Two70, then discuss what we had read over dessert. I was excited to see what she had offered me.

So, reclining together, the two of us read our books in comfortable silence. The time flew by, and I barely finished five chapters by the time we were ready to leave. We ordered two molten lava cakes with glasses of milk.

"So," she began, "what do you think so far?"

I thought about it.

I smiled and nodded; this girl was perfect.

When our desserts came, Heidi moved to sit with me in my booth. We sat like lovers, eating our chocolate cakes and leaving our milk mustaches like a couple of kids. The girl made me giddy, and I ate slowly because I didn't want it to end. But it's pretty hard to make a hot chocolate lava cake last, and soon it was time for bed.

∞

An hour later I was in bed in the stateroom, my book in my hand. I briefly thought about the day: the dinner plans for Saturday were written in stone, my parents eager and agreeable to the time. Heidi and I had a full schedule for the following day; my heart was heavy over leaving the girl who had saved my cruise.

"Better get reading, Bud," I mumbled softly to myself. "There's no time to waste."

I opened the book, laid my bookmark on the nightstand, and began.

CHAPTER 14

"Tripp, honey, are you awake in there?"

My mother's voice cut through my dreams, startling me awake. I opened my eyes wide and jumped from my slumber. What time was it? One look at the clock told me I had forgotten to set my alarm. It was nine twenty-two; I should have met Heidi for breakfast at the Icon at nine.

"Yeah! Yeah, Mom! I'm up!"

I jumped up and started pulling my jeans on in a panic.

"Good. Your friend Heidi is here," Mom yelled. "I'll let her know."

I cursed myself as I struggled, half-asleep, to dress. I had to take my t-shirt off twice and turn it right-side out. The first time it was right, but I was still too asleep and thought it wasn't; I ended up turning it inside-out, realized it once it was on, and had to do it all over again.

I brushed my hair and teeth, washed my face in the forsaken AquaSim, and put my feet in my tennis shoes without untying them, which ended up taking longer than if I had done it right, to begin with. I was running around my little room like a chicken with its head cut off.

At last, I flung open my door to see Heidi and my parents, sitting comfortably and laughing easily together.

"Hi… good morning, I mean." I grinned sheepishly at the glowing girl before me. "I, uh, overslept."

"I see that." She stood up and offered her hand to my mother. "It was good to meet you officially and chat finally." They had barely met in passing. I was almost glad I overslept.

My eyes were still a bit gritty from sleep. I took the time to quickly rub them and shake my head hard, trying to get alert faster. Before I knew it, Heidi was saying, "Ready?"

It was all I could do to smile and nod at my parents, and I decided that I would have coffee for breakfast. I had slept hard; coming back to life on such short notice was proving to be quite a task. Even walking to the elevator, with Heidi steering me by the hand, I was groggy.

The elevator doors closed and we started up. "You look hit, Tripp!" she teased. "Did you sneak some booze before bed?"

She was smiling in fun, but I gave her a 'ha, funny' smirk, which made her laugh aloud. "Good sleep, then?"

"Oh, man, I'm telling you." I looked at my shoes and shook my head; now my right shoe was all the way untied. "I forgot to set my alarm. If you hadn't come I would have slept through lunch, I think."

She stroked my shoulders with her hand and kissed

my cheek. "No worries. You could java up; the day marches on."

As it turned out, I sucked down three cups of coffee in rapid succession, and soon she couldn't shut me up. I was enthusiastically giving her my report on what I had read so far in my book; I was talking with my hands and enunciating like a madman.

After a while, I paused for a drink. With an amused smile, Heidi teased, "So, you like it, then? Because you lost me after, 'Oh, yeah! I read a lot of that book.' "

I realized how fast I had been talking and got a vision of what I must have looked like, long monkey arms swinging around and my mouth stretched across my face in a corny smile. I almost choked and spit my drink out from the visual, and when I safely got the drink down, I lost it hysterically.

For the next five minutes, we laughed so hard that people stared. I had tears running down my face like I had spigots in my eyes, and I could hardly breathe. Every time I almost got it under control, I would think of some stupid thing I said, and how I looked saying it, and I would lose it again. Everyone in the Icon was craning their necks and looking at us as if we were on drugs or something.

By the time it stopped, we both realized our French toast breakfasts were on the table. Heidi looked at her plate, then at me, and said, "That poor server probably ran for their life."

We broke out again, but this time it was far more subdued. It felt just as good though, and I had to touch her. I reached across the table and took her hand; it was soft, warm, and dry.

"I don't want to leave you," I whispered.

Heidi stared into my eyes, the corners of her mouth turned up slightly, the after-effect of the laughter. "I don't know what to do." She whispered back.

After an electric, yet a bittersweet moment, Heidi gently took her hand from mine. She lifted my plate and set it before me, putting my milk in position, and doing the same with my plate of sausages; she did the same with her own meal.

I watched her without touching my food. When she had everything just right she looked up at me and smiled fully, her eyes bright. "Now, let's eat."

Pulling myself together, I began.

"So how do you like your book?" I asked her. "Well, so far I love it."

Heidi grinned, a reminiscent look on her face.

We talked, and what followed for the next two hours, was one of the most intelligent, heartfelt conversations of my life. It consisted of honesty, trust, understanding, and true mental intimacy. I have never had a conversation like it since.

We blew off our plans of shopping without even thinking about it. The concept of time didn't exist, and neither of us wanted it to end. But the restlessness of adolescence soon rudely interrupted, and the intensity of the topic began to run its course.

"Wow," I almost shouted. "It's almost noon! We wasted the entire morning."

"Tripp, if you think this was a waste we're on the wrong page." I looked at her face, thinking she was angry with my lack of thoughtfulness, but she was smiling. "How about this: for the rest of this cruise we focus less on what we are doing and more on the person we are doing it with. Let's walk and talk! And what crosses our paths and lures us—we'll do. But right now is all we have as far as we know. All these plans, well, they are distracting us. Let's not waste it."

Heidi stood up, took me by the hand, and pulled me to my feet. Wrapping her arm around my waist, she snuggled me, and we began to slowly walk. She gave me a squeeze.

R.W.K. Clark

CHAPTER 15

Once I listened to Heidi's words at breakfast, and let them sink in, things changed for me as far as the quality of my time with her. I stopped trying to cram years of living into two weeks, and I focused on her alone. Suddenly, I didn't obsess in the back of my mind on the fact we were docking in a few days; I stopped counting the seconds and minutes. Instead, I lived in the moment. It changed everything.

We grew close very quickly, at a pace nothing like before.

The only things I can remember about the next few hours of that day, until early afternoon, were Heidi and the words she said. I remember every funny story, every last laugh, and every tear that snuck down her face. I memorized the way she looked, smelled, sounded, and felt. I ingrained the taste of her mouth into my brain.

We did nothing but walk until three; we didn't stop for lunch, and we paid no mind to the activities available around us. I couldn't tell you what decks we strolled, or the order we took them in. I can't recall any specific persons or faces at all. Actually, when I pull up my mental file for that memory, it seems no one was around us; it's as if we were on that massive boat all alone.

It must have been between two-thirty and three when we plopped down on a couple of deck chairs, both of us letting out long relaxing sighs and falling into a comfortable silence. After a long while, Heidi turned her head to me casually; I was watching her profile for several minutes, and she had simply lain back and quietly basked in the attention.

When she looked at me, she spoke in a low voice. "I wish there was a place under the open sky where we could go at night, a place on the ship that is sort of isolated. Where we wouldn't be bothered."

"Where we could sleep under the stars together all night, and no one would wake us but the sun," I finished.

She sat up abruptly, her entire face smiling. She was excited. "Yes!" She was almost whispering now. Her eyes darted around wildly; she didn't want anyone but me to hear her words. "I wonder if there is?"

"We have balconies; we could hang on one of them." I was whispering back.

Now Heidi shook her head vigorously. "No! I mean a place somewhere, on a deck. Away from moms and dads and passengers. A place where no one could see us at all, but we would be completely out in the open. I wonder if there is a way to find out?"

I thought about it; it would be incredible to sleep all night in her arms, smelling her hair and kissing her soft lips. All of a sudden my mind started to go crazy. Was there someplace on board like that, a place we could hide for a night under the moon and stars?

"For starters, we could look at the deck plans. I bet they have them in the library," I mused.

She jumped up and grabbed my hand. "Let's get a hot dog and go find out."

Soon, she was pulling me enthusiastically toward the elevator.

∞

The ship's library was comfortable but small. The plans for the 'Diamond of the Seas' cruise ship were available for passengers, for study inside the library.

The place was quiet, and from what I could see, Heidi and I were the only visitors. We sat at a long table which was positioned against a wall. A single lamp was stationed on the opposite side, directly in the middle. It illuminated the pages of the long, rectangular hardback in which pages of the ship's deck plans were bound, from Deck 3-16.

We studied them together, one-by-one, quietly. If we spoke to point something out or to ask a question, it was in a whisper. Mostly we both focused on reading and identifying each and every thing featured before us, beginning with Deck 3.

About halfway through our research, Heidi suddenly stopped. She sat back in her chair, and I could feel her eyes on my head. I turned to see what she was doing.

"What?" I asked.

She had a devilish little grin on her face and a twinkle in her eye to match. With a turn of her head to the right, then the left, she checked to see if the coast was clear. Turning back to me, she wrinkled up her nose the way I adored.

"How do you feel about playing grown-ups?" she whispered, her tone conspiratorial, her expression full of shenanigans.

I was instantly confused. "Play grown-ups? What does that have to do with sleeping under the stars?"

Heidi looked around again and held her finger to her lips; I was talking out loud. "I want to go into the Solarium and sleep in deck chairs, watching the water and sky."

I thought about it for a minute. The Solarium was an adults-only pool area with a pool, hot tubs, a bar, and comfortable deck chairs with thick cushions. It was enclosed under a dome-like glass structure, so the temperature there usually remained the same: nice and warm, as opposed to the cold night air outside. It was a brilliant solution. It would keep us from getting into trouble sneaking around in restricted areas, and we would be comfortable.

"The only problem might be if, as it gets late, one of the crew starts to question us," I thought aloud. "Might want to call our parents."

"So, we tell them we're eighteen." It sounded like she had already made a firm decision. "Either of us passes for it, and they'll never make us go back to our stateroom for our identification. Just wear something… a bit more mature."

"Like what?"

Heidi rolled her eyes. "Something old people wear. You wear khakis and a polo. You have something like that, don't you?"

I thought about it. "No, but my dad does. We're the same height, but I weigh a little more."

"Good!" she exclaimed. "You should fill it out nicely. I'm going to wear a sundress. We'll look just fine. Oh, I'd better bring a shawl, just in case I get a chill. I won't sleep well without some kind of covers."

I sat back in my chair and breathed a sigh of relief; no sneaking around! "So, what night do you want to do this?"

"Our last night here," she replied softly. "After the Festival of Hues. We can find some loungers away from the bar. Everyone will be getting ready to dock. It will be perfect, and the ocean will be in front of us." She went still, pondering for a moment, then looked up at me with large, sad eyes.

"Do you know what I miss the most about the world before?" she asked, and I gently shook my head. "The dolphins. I miss the dolphins the most."

I put my arms around her shoulders, pulling her to me, and she laid her head against my shoulder. It looked like we would actually get to spend a night together, I missed the dolphins all the time too. They sure had been a sight.

CHAPTER 16

With something brand new to look forward to, I also felt we were getting something valuable to remember. No, sex wasn't involved. If it happened somehow, it happened. But getting to hold Heidi in my arms all night long was something I wanted to commemorate. I decided, while in bed that night, that I would purchase something special for her.

It was a good thing I got such good sleep the night before because once I got the gift idea in my head, I hardly got a wink of sleep. I wound up tossing and turning so much that I finally threw in the towel and got up. I went through the complimentary magazine rack in the sitting area, lights on dim and quiet as a mouse, looking for the little flyers they had that detailed the shopping opportunities on board. I needed to figure out what was even available, other than some sort of cheesy souvenir.

The first three pamphlets were for Bulgari, Regalia, and some other shop I couldn't pronounce. Quick glances through told me none of them would have what I wanted, not to mention the fact that their prices were atrocious. I didn't know exactly what I wanted, but I believed I would know it when I saw it.

I pawed through the magazine rack some more. It seemed to be nothing but lists of available dining places, activities, and the like. I almost lost hope, but there was one more thing, crumpled at the very bottom. I fished it out with little expectation.

It was a tiny, all-inclusive catalog about a little boutique on board called 'Shadowfly.' It sounded like a fishing enthusiast's place, so I half-heartedly flipped the pages, landing on page three. It was the first thing my eyes landed on.

It was a gold ring. The first stone, a large, blue oval, was an aquamarine, according to the brief description given. Next to it was a smaller, three-quarter carat diamond. The gold ring itself was shaped into two dolphins, which appeared to be playing ball with the stones. It couldn't have been more perfect.

I squinted at the price: $425 USD. Well, I didn't have that kind of cash just lying around, and I wouldn't borrow it from my dad. But what I did have was a college fund, tucked safely away in the bank, and I had a credit card hooked to that account which was strictly for emergencies. I had never used it, but I had never needed to, either.

I thought about it for a fraction of a second: this was sort of an emergency, and I had no qualms whatsoever about borrowing money from myself.

I took the tiny leaflet into my room with me and, checking my alarm, I changed it. I needed to get up an hour earlier. Heidi and I were meeting at nine, but we weren't eating together. Her father and mother wanted her to have breakfast with them. I had been bummed, but, I had been hogging her time.

Now, however, I would have the smallest window of free time in which to go see if Shadowfly was still carrying the ring. I hoped, but even if it wasn't, I had faith I would find her something. I would get up, shower, and be at the shop by opening time: eight o'clock in the morning.

I fell asleep with a smile on my face, thinking of sitting her down for an iced coffee when we met up and giving her my gift. I was out fast, dreams of her in my head. I remember clearly how sweet my sleep was that night, and I can almost weep.

∞

"How was the breakfast?"

Heidi was just sitting down on a stool next to me at Icon. A cold caramel iced coffee sat waiting for her, and I was sipping one of my own. I opted for the stools at the bar just to start; I wanted her to be able to see me right away when she came in.

"Good," she replied as she made herself comfortable on the stool. "Fruit and whole-grain waffles. Definitely not French toast." She grinned and took a long drink of the coffee. After licking her very prominent mustache away, she turned to me smiling. "Why the change of plans? Thought you wanted to meet at the track. Something come up early?"

I glanced around the room. "Let's get a booth, huh? There's one in the corner there. That way we can talk."

She stood and grabbed her coffee, but she had a concerned look. "Is everything okay? Did something happen?"

"No!" I stopped and shook my head. "No way! I just wanted to sit away from everyone. Oh! You mean the change of plans?" I started walking again, and she followed me. "I just had something to do, and I thought the coffee sounded good, so I slipped the note under your door. You don't mind, do you?"

She shook her head and smiled with relief. Once we were settled once again, she asked, "How did you sleep?"

Rising out of her seat, she came around and squeezed in with me. I loved the move; it made me feel wanted. As soon as she sat she planted a long kiss on my cheek, grabbed her coffee, and settled back.

"So, the sleep?"

I couldn't help but chuckle at her behavior. "Oh, mine, it was good. Had a little trouble at first, but once I finally went to sleep, I slept hard."

"Me, too," she replied. "And sorry about the note, I didn't want to wake your mom and dad."

"Naw. They sleep like the dead."

She took me by the hand and began to drink her coffee in silence; I tried to do the same.

It wasn't long before I was thinking too much, and my nerves got the best of me. I began to squirm a little, but soon it was a full-blown fidget. Next thing I knew I started scratching itches that weren't there.

"Tripp, what the heck?"

I took a deep breath; I was letting my nerves get the better of me. It wasn't like I was asking her to marry me or anything. I was just giving her a gift, a memento. Just a little something to remember me by.

"Heidi, would you just… sit back across the table for a minute?" I asked. It would be easier to look at her and talk if she were over there.

A weird look came over her face like she really thought something was wrong with me. She stood up but kept her eyes on me as she moved back to her original seat. She didn't move her coffee this time; it sat, forgotten, on my side of the table.

"Okay," she said slowly, "I moved. I take it this is serious if you don't even want to sit next to me."

I understood the look she was giving me all at once; she thought I was going to sort of 'break it off' with her, or tell her I didn't want to hang out! She was concerned I was trying to let her down easy! I started to laugh, and the look of relief that came over her face was priceless.

She chuckled softly, her eyes still searching mine. "I just wanted to talk, and it's easier if I can see you without wrenching my neck."

"So, talk."

Time for another deep breath. "Well, I just wanted to tell you that the time I have spent with you has been awesome. And I know that we live a good distance from each other, but I really, really hope that we keep in touch and that we can get together someday." I started to feel a bit more confident, slowly but surely. "I mean, if I give you my number and address, I hope you write or call or something, but I understand if this sort of 'slips away' after we dock."

"You know that if I have your number, I'll call," she said in an encouraging voice. "I don't want this to end just because the cruise ends. You know, we both might be in high school, but I don't have a steady boyfriend at home. Sure, I've dated, but I'm not in love with anyone. At least, I wasn't… until now."

I almost didn't catch it. I was so preoccupied with the fact that she said she would keep in touch that the last thing she said almost slipped right by me. Then it seemed my mind sorted it out all of a sudden. I felt my eyes widen.

"Did you say you love me again?"

She nodded shyly and looked down at her hands in her lap, a little smile on her lips.

"I love you too."

I reached into my front pants pocket and wrapped my hand around the small box inside. I tried to be nonchalant, to pull it out without her really paying me any mind. The best way to do that, I knew, would be to start talking.

"So, you will call me? I mean, when you get home, you'll stay in touch? You promise?"

"I promise, Tripp. I would really like to see how far this relationship can go." She looked me directly in the eyes, and I could see that she truly cared; her love was real.

I had the ring box under the table now, and I opened the lid. It took a second to pull it out and set it on the table before her. I watched her mouth drop open, and I sat back, enjoying the moment immensely.

"Is this for me?"

I gave her a nod, and she took the ring from its velvet-lined case gently. "They're dolphins."

"Yes," I replied. "Dolphins."

She had tears in her eyes when she looked at me again. "So, are you—?"

"This isn't a proposal," I said quickly. "We aren't ready for that. This is something you can remember me by, and remember our time together. It's a way for me to say, she was my girlfriend, if only for a minute."

Heidi held the ring out to me. "Will you put it on me?"

I took it, and she held out her left hand. I was so worried that it wouldn't fit; I had guessed on her size and settled on size six because it looked right. When I slid it on her third finger, which she was holding out for the ring, it slid on nicely.

Tears fell down her cheeks as she gazed at her hand, holding it proudly out in front of her face. "It's beautiful," she murmured, then she looked back at me. "I'll still be your girlfriend when this is over. We'll keep in touch; we'll make it work, you'll see. It will take time, but if you care about me the same as I do for you, it will work."

For the fourth time since she arrived, Heidi rose and moved to sit next to me. We embraced, and soon we were kissing like a couple of newlyweds. Other people could have been staring or pointing, but if they were, neither of us took any notice. It felt good, it felt right, and it felt like we were meant to be.

After a short time, I released her and sat back against the wall. "Are you hungry, or did the fruit and stuff fill you up?"

"I'm fine. How about you?"

I shrugged. "Food is really the last thing on my mind. Do you want to get out of here? I thought maybe we could visit the Solarium and stake out our spots for our sleepover. Are you game?"

With a quick, happy nod of her head, we left the Icon and made our way to Deck 14. We decided to walk and take the stairs rather than catch an elevator. It would give us time together that we wouldn't have any other way.

The Solarium wasn't packed, by any means, but there were several passengers around. Some at the pool, several at the bar, and a smattering seated here and there in deck chairs, either talking or taking in the view of the colored waters. We walked around slowly for a while, but I didn't see any spot worthy of spending the night away from people. I was about to suggest we just tell our parents we wanted to sleep on the balcony again when she grabbed my arm.

"Over there," she pointed.

I followed her forefinger to see four deck chairs facing the dome. The water was stretched out before them endlessly, and it almost looked like you were right on top of it, steering the ship from the front seat. It was nothing short of amazing.

"Now to hope that no one takes them before we get here after the festival," I mused. "Make sure you have your things packed for docking before the festival; that way you don't have to worry about it in the morning."

"I know. I told you that, remember?" She gave my arm a sock.

I thought about it for a minute. "Maybe we should come up with backup seats, you know. Just in case."

Heidi agreed, and we started walking again. "Remember," she said, "most all of the passengers are going to be staying in after the festival; there aren't going to be many here, I don't think. At least, not as many as usual."

"Are you going to tell your parents what we plan to do?" I asked.

She didn't hesitate. "Yes. Are you?"

"Well, if you are, I am." I chuckled. "It wouldn't look good if you were the only one in this who is willing to 'man up.' Will they be okay with it?"

She gave my hand a squeeze. "My mom and dad trust me. If I tell them we are sleeping on the deck they may ask about sex, or hint around about it out of concern, but—" she paused, stopped walking, and turned to me. "But you should know that I took a vow of celibacy, you know until I marry. So, I hope this isn't about sex."

"Heidi, I would never pressure you. We don't even have to kiss; I just want to be with you."

She kissed me then, and we started walking again. "Don't think you won't be kissing me," she teased. "I

139

actually planned on some hot making out." She gave me a wink.

"How about over there?" I gestured toward a row of seven deck chairs; they didn't have the same great view, but they were sort of hidden from the bar. "This would do as a backup plan, I guess."

"Well, even if people are in any of the chairs we want, they won't be there all night, and we will," she pointed out. "I think we're good, don't you?"

"It's a date," I agreed.

As we were leaving, I gave the clock over the bar a look. "It's almost eleven. What do you want for lunch?"

She wrapped her arm around my waist. "I don't care; you choose. Surprise me."

CHAPTER 17

A comedian was performing at the Royal Theater that night, followed by an old '70s rock band that my dad loved. I had heard their music growing up, and I loved comedy, so after we ate, I asked Heidi if that sounded like a good time.

The show started at seven. The comedian would take an hour, then the band would play for two. We would eat dinner there during the show, and we would be able to have fun at the same time, all in one place. She thought it was a great idea.

We both decided to take the afternoon to talk to our parents about our plans at the Solarium that afternoon. We agreed that the sooner we brought it up, the more time we would have to deal with any objections in time for Saturday night and the festival. I didn't think my parents would put up a fight, but I was sure I would get a lecture on personal sexual responsibility from my dad. He didn't say much, but when he did, he laid it on thick.

As for Heidi, she didn't think her parents would hassle her at all. She mentioned that she might have to agree on them quietly dropping in to 'look in' on us, but I didn't have a problem with that. I actually thought it was a great bargaining tool if my own mom and dad put up a stink. So, we went our separate ways around three, and I agreed to pick her up at her stateroom at six-thirty for the show.

When I arrived at my stateroom I could hear the television through the door; my parents were there. I took one of my now-common deep breaths and walked in. I had also decided to tell my dad about the money I took out of my college fund for Heidi's ring, so I was a bit nervous, to say the least.

"Hey, Dad," I said cheerfully as I closed the door behind me. After a quick look around I asked, "Where's Mom?"

He turned to look at me. "Oh, hey, Tripp. She's in the shower. What's up?"

I plopped down, as casually as I could, into a chair. "Well, I need to talk to you, but it really needs to be both of you. So, we can wait. What are you watching?"

It turned out to be an old '80s movie, and my question immediately prompted my father to begin giving me the entire professional history of this one-time popular actor and martial artist. It wasn't the first time; if any '80s action star came on TV, I was subjected to an instant, unwanted education on their biography.

Just when I started thinking about hanging myself to escape the torture, my mother appeared. "Hi, Tripp! I didn't think we'd see you until this evening. Something wrong?"

"The boy needs to talk to us, Kate," my father grumbled, annoyed that his narrative had been interrupted.

"Oh?" She poured a cup of coffee from the small pot behind the bar, then sat next to my father on the sofa. "Go ahead; we're all ears."

Immediately, I thought to myself, 'Now what? Why didn't you rehearse all this in your head?' My hands started to fidget, and I squirmed a little bit, but they sat quietly and waited with patience.

"Well," I began, "I guess for starters I wanted to talk to you about Heidi." It would be best to bring up the Solarium stay first; if I brought up the money first, my dad might blow a fuse. Then he would say no to my night with Heidi automatically. "You know how we are having supper on Saturday with Heidi and her folks?" They nodded. "And how we are going to the Festival of Hues after?" Another nod. "Well, since it will be our last night before docking, we made some plans together for late into the night."

"What kind of plans?" This was my mom; she didn't miss a beat.

My fidgeting doubled. "Well, we kind of plan on sleeping, overnight, in the Solarium. You know, to watch the stars."

I braced myself, but neither of them spoke. They were staring at me, almost as if they were trying to listen to someone interpret a foreign language for them. I groaned inwardly.

"So," Mom said, "you and your sixteen or seventeen-year-old girlfriend want to spend your last night together sleeping in a public space, on a secure cruise ship, with crew members all around? What, holding hands and occasionally kissing when you're not sleeping?"

I gave her a sheepish grin and shrugged.

My mother turned to my father, but he was still staring at me and didn't notice. She continued. "I don't see a problem with it; make sure you both have a couple of blankets. If anyone from the crew gives you trouble, tell them to talk to us."

She stood and walked back to the coffee pot for more java; I just sat there in stunned silence.

"Kate! What do you mean? They are kids!" My dad's voice was raised slightly, and he was looking at my mother as if she had grown a third arm. I just kept my trap shut.

"Look, Jim. This has been a hard time for everyone; the only thing these two kids have really had is each other." She looked at her coffee while she stirred it. "Have you ever known Tripp to make an irresponsible decision? I mean, look, he even came and told us about this! He didn't sneak off or make us worry, or worse yet, lie."

They both looked back to me expectantly; time to talk. "Listen, if you are worried about sex, you should know that we realize this may be the last time we see each other. Having sex could mean a baby; then what? Not to mention the fact that Heidi took a vow of celibacy until marriage; she would never break it, and I would never ask her to."

My dad's face softened a bit, and he gave my mother

a glance. I continued. "This may be the last time we ever see each other; they live in Miami Beach. We promised to stay in contact; hopefully, we both have something in the future. Time will tell. So, can I?"

"I said yes," my mother repeated. "Say yes, Jim."

"Yes," he muttered as he sat back on the sofa, still staring at me.

"And that brings me to my next subject. You know how I said we promised to keep in touch?" I waited for acknowledgment, but they both just looked at me. "Um, well, we also promised each other that we would be committed... you know, to make it work. We, um, love each other."

"Now, Tripp, you've only been on the boat for ten days, Son." Mom sat back down. "I understand how strong adolescent affection can be, but trust me, as someone who has lived it, it can be just as fleeting."

"I love her, Mom," I repeated. "We are not going to run away together. We are going to continue our lives and stay in close contact. But we said our promises; I'm going to keep them, and I believe she will, too."

My fidgeting now tripled.

"So, I bought her a ring out of my college fund." There, I said it.

I don't know if I thought a bomb would go off immediately or what. I actually closed my eyes in expectation, but the room went dead still. I waited and finally opened my eyes to see their faces. That was all it took; as soon as I showed him my pupils, he went off the deep end. But it wasn't like a bomb; it was like a madman ready to go on a spree: quietly furious. This was bad.

"What did you say?" My father's voice was low and even.

My mother put her coffee down and placed her hand on his left shoulder, after which she began to stroke it softly. She covered her mouth with the back of her hand and pretended to look intently at the floor. Her body language loudly said, 'This is a job for Jim.'

"I said, I bought a ring for Heidi with money from my college fund?" It came out like a question, and my voice even squeaked a little. My dad was pissed.

I thought I saw a little steam come from his ears. In a voice that was almost a whisper, he said, "How much?"

"Four hundred and twenty-five plus tax." I held my breath.

He actually looked like he might have sighed in relief. When he spoke again, his voice was closer to normal, but he still held me tightly with his eyes. I didn't know what to expect.

"Okay," he began. "It could have been much worse; actually, I expected it. This can be fixed. You'll pay it back."

"Of course, Dad."

"I don't suppose you thought about the fact that your mother and I have been going through some perspective changes." He paused, then asked, "Did you?"

After a slight nod, I replied, "Um, yes."

He nodded back. "You knew. I don't suppose you considered that making these changes would include our changing jobs, did you? Or that that kind of change could possibly cause us to rein in our finances, huh, Tripp?"

Now I just sat there, because to answer could mean death. It was lecture time, pure and simple, and I had to take it because I had screwed up. At least it wasn't the sex lecture.

"Give me the bank card," he said simply, then clucked his tongue and shook his head. "Never thought I'd see the day."

He held his hand out in waiting as I pulled out my wallet and fished out the demon bank card that wouldn't be in my possession for the foreseeable future. I handed it over quickly, then busied myself with putting my wallet back.

"I'll keep this until the debt is paid back," he continued. "I'll be deducting ten dollars from your weekly chore allowance, and you can mow, wash the car until it disappears." He looked at me for a long moment, then gave me a half-hearted smile and a chuckle. "She is a cutie, Son; I have to admit it. If I were you, there's no telling how badly I would have screwed up. Now go on, go about your business."

"Thank you." I jumped up like my rear end was on fire and shut myself in my room fast. I fell backward onto my bed and exhaled long and hard. I really dodged a bullet, and I was glad I had decided to come clean. If my dad had seen the discrepancy without my having told him beforehand, and he would have eventually, he would have really, and I mean really punished me. I would've never gotten a car for my eighteenth birthday; he would have made me earn the money myself, guaranteed. Good call, old chap, I thought to myself.

A quick look to my nightstand clock told me it was four-fifteen; there were two more hours until I would pick up Heidi. A nap sounded good; all of a sudden, I felt drained, and I knew it was because of the stress of 'the talk.' I would take a nap, then wake up refreshed for the evening. I set the alarm for five-thirty and got snug under the covers.

I lay there smiling; I had a full evening with my girl ahead.

∞

I was sitting in the sand on a beach; the sun was shining brightly, glistening like diamonds on the tiny grains beneath me. I wondered why I hadn't brought a towel to sit on; the grains were digging into my palms, and I probably would get some in my shorts. I turned my face toward the sun, the towel forgotten.

Laughter came to my ears, and for the first time, I looked toward the water. It was a stunning turquoise blue, so sharp that it almost made the sand look white. It was insanely clear, and I could see all of the fish and dolphins and whales swimming in it. It was almost as if they were in an aquarium right before my eyes.

I heard laughter again, I turned in the direction it came from, and there was Heidi, running and laughing in the sand. She wasn't in the water, but she was right alongside it. She wore a yellow bikini, the shade that looked best with her hair, and her hair flowed free, blowing behind her in long spirals as she ran.

She turned and ran back in my direction, arms in the sun. She wore big sunglasses, and the smile on her face was wide; she looked happy and free, and it made me laugh. I watched her, taking pleasure in her pleasure.

"Tripp, come on!" she yelled suddenly. "It's so blue!"

She began to spin in circles. I laughed louder then and stood up to go meet her. I was about halfway to her when she yelled, "I'm going in!" She took off at full speed for the water.

I continued to make my way to her, watching her as she ran. Something caught my eye in the water to her right, and I turned quickly. A massive whale, or at least its corpse, broke the surface of the water, bobbed for a moment, then settled. A fish came up next, then a seal.

I began to jog. "Heidi, stop! Wait! Don't go in yet!"

But she didn't seem to hear me. Now all kinds of sea life were appearing, some bloated, all dead. I began to run as fast as I could, and Heidi did too. I couldn't catch up, and I was screaming over and over for her to stop. No matter how fast I ran, I couldn't catch up to her.

Right before she reached the water's edge, the sea began to change. Sludgy oranges and greens with red and purple swirls began to bubble and churn. I turned to Heidi, screaming louder. She reached the water and leapt, as though trying to jump as far in as she could.

In mid-air, she heard me and turned…

I sat straight up and cried out; I was panting, and my clothes were soaked with sweat.

The blankets I had covered up with were in a wad at the foot of the bed, and both pillows were on the floor. The light from the windows was dim; I had closed the blinds almost all the way that morning, and now I could hardly see. I reached over, fumbling, and turned on the lamp on my nightstand.

The clock said four fifty-eight; I had been asleep a little more than a half-hour. Leaning my head back, I closed my eyes and let myself breath in and out. The dream was still clear in my mind, and I wanted to rid myself of its burden so it wouldn't affect my mood.

But the vision of the whale bodies popping to the surface, and the sea changing color before my very eyes, wouldn't leave my head. The sound of Heidi's laughter ripped at my heart, and in my waking state, it was overwhelming. I sat in the middle of the bed, pulled my knees up to my chest like a scared, lost little boy, and cried like a baby, my face buried in my blanket-clad knees.

I just let it happen. I didn't try to fight it. It was obvious to me, even as I sat there sobbing my head off. I had needed to do it for a long time, and I was just glad it all came bursting out when I was alone in my room. The weeping was the best thing for me, and I just let it pour its way out of my system.

It took about fifteen minutes. I went from crying so hard I could barely breathe, to crying, then stopping, then crying again. Soon, I was just breathing hard and sniffling. I looked at the clock again: five-twenty-two. With a flip of the switch on top of the clock, I shut off the alarm and swung my legs to the floor. There was no reason to sit there any longer; may as well shower and get ready. I was picking Heidi up at six-thirty.

The shower proved to do more than cleanse my body; it also cleared many of the details of the dream from my mind. By the time I got out and began drying off, the only things left of my sleeping vision were tiny fragments, and my emotions felt nothing more than a fraction of a second's tug. It would pass.

CHAPTER 18

Since our date consisted of a comedian and an old rock and roll band, I opted to wear a newer pair of jeans, a black silk collared shirt, and loafers. I doused myself lightly in aftershave and took extra time on my hair. Before long I was freshly shaved, showered, and looking good if I did say so myself. I wondered what Heidi would wear, not because I cared too much about fashion, but because she looked so good all the time. I was anxious to see her beautiful face (and the rest of her) again.

I walked out of my room to see my dad sitting at the small dining table, and my mother taking food from someone at the door. They were getting ready to sit down to dinner, and the smell of the food suddenly made my stomach rumble. She looked up at me and smiled.

"Good nap?"

I nodded and offered her a smile back, feeling a twinge of guilt about my little white lie.

"Sorry, Tripp," she continued as she sat down across from my dad. "Did you want me to order something for you?"

"No," I replied. "Heidi and I are going to see a comedian at the Royal Theater; we'll eat there. But thanks. Don't mind me; I'm just going to sit here and watch TV. I'm not leaving for a few minutes."

While they ate, I sat and stared at the TV: some kind of documentary about the Titanic was playing (how appropriate), and I just wasn't into it. I really didn't care to work myself back up, or in any way think about the water, or the cruise, or the state of the planet. I just wanted to pass the time.

My dad said, "I didn't know that a comedian was playing tonight. I mean, I knew they had some shows, but I should have paid better attention to their show times. Kate, that's going to be a good show."

"Remember when we went to see that one comedian?" she asked him.

Both of them burst out laughing, and out of the corner of my eye, I could see my mother was blushing a deep red. "Must have been a heck of a night, Mom."

She waved her hand at me, embarrassed. "Forget about all that, Tripp. You are going to enjoy it."

I shook my head, wondering what they did together the night they saw a comedian.

While I truly loved my parents, and I felt great to see them flirting and reminiscing and blushing, I felt uncomfortable. I was their sixteen-year-old son, and no teenager likes the thought of their parents, you know, making googly-eyes or getting romantic, not to mention having sex… ewww!

It was enough to drive me out the door ten minutes

early, with a quick kiss to my mother's cheek and a slap to my father's shoulder. Best to let them be alone before they decided to get any 'fun and games' started. I would simply take my time on the way to Heidi's stateroom.

If I took the elevator, depending on how busy it was, I would be there in, like, three minutes. I decided to take the stairs, and though I felt like hustling, I fought against the urge. I wanted to be calm and confident around her, not sweating and puffing with tousled hair. So, I strolled.

I knocked on her door at exactly six-thirty, and she answered it almost as soon as my knuckles hit it the first time. We both started laughing; it was obvious we were anxious to see each other, and we both caught the comedy of it.

"Good. You're here," she whispered. She stood on her toes and kissed my cheek softly, and for a long moment. I closed my eyes to enjoy the feel of her lips, and I inhaled the strawberry scent on her hair deeply.

I stepped into the stateroom, and Heidi softly closed the door behind me. "Hi, Mr. and Mrs. Collins. How are you this evening?"

"Tripp! Hi!" Mr. Collins was smiling. "Heidi tells us you two are going to see a comedian."

I nodded and chuckled. "My dad says we'll enjoy it. We'll see." I was teasing, and by the Collins' laughter at my statement, I could tell they knew it.

"You will." Mrs. Collins added her two cents.

Back to Ted, who glanced at his watch. "Anyway, looking forward to dinner, Tripp; excited to meet your folks. You two better get going; you'll want to get a good table."

We left hand in hand. The first thing Heidi said was, "Sorry about them; they're big dorks."

"Yeah, well, you should have seen mine," I told her. "Just the mention of a comedian and they were ready to strip down and get busy."

She laughed loudly. "No way!"

"No kidding. It was embarrassing." I squeezed her hand.

Heidi shook her head. "Well, let's have fun, shall we?"

To be honest, I didn't care if we were going to spend three hours watching camels mate, as long as we did it together.

∞

The comedian was hilarious. He could be a bit vulgar, and he cursed a lot, but his jokes were right on target, and he had us cracking up almost the entire time. Our dinner was served during his gig, and I will admit that most of ours went cold; the guy was too funny.

We both ordered rotini with long Italian sausage links, served with buttered green beans. For dessert we had warm, ice cream-topped brownies; those went down way too easily. I will also say that we overdosed on soda pops, drinking them down one after another until we were both jittery from the caffeine.

By the time the band started, we were full and happy, and we were able to sit back and really listen to the music. Much of their stuff was harder rock; kids my age usually listened to techno or pop, but the words were awesome and meaningful, something our music lacked. I was familiar with more of their work than I realized, and even Heidi got excited on two occasions, saying, 'I know this one!'

It was a great time, and we felt like a couple of grown-ups. We left the Royal laughing, recalling jokes and singing the lyrics to the songs we heard. Both of us had fun emulating the band members; it was a riot to see old, gray-haired men jamming out like kids. Sure, they moved a bit stiffly, at least I could tell, but they were having fun, and they put on a good show, for a bunch of old codgers.

"Do you think when we have kids they'll think our music is goofy?" Heidi asked suddenly.

We had just arrived at our favorite spot on Deck 16, and we were just settling into a couple of loungers. Her question took me by surprise, and I stopped situating myself, freezing dead in my tracks. Had she just asked me about 'our' kids?

"Tripp, did you hear me?"

I looked over at her. She was already lying back, nice and relaxed. Heidi had worn what had come to be my favorite item of her clothing: her yellow and orange sundress. Right then, at ten-thirty at night, the moon was bright over us, and it lit her up like a star.

"Tripp? Hello?"

I chuckled and lay back. "You think we might have kids?"

"We could," she replied. "I mean, we both made

promises about working to keep our relationship. If we mean them, maybe we should think and talk like it's all going to happen just the way we want it to."

I liked that. "Yeah, I do. I think our kids are going to see us as the biggest dorks in the world. But hey, maybe not. Maybe that is the reason our folks look that way to us. We're super-cool. They will want to be just like us."

"Right, ha-ha." She leaned up on her elbow. "Hey, come lie by me."

I turned to her, startled. "On your lounger?"

She gave me a look. "No, goofy, on the deck next to my lounger. Of course, on my lounger! What's wrong? You don't want to?"

I jumped up like a flash and did as I was told. Heidi lay in the crook of my arm, both of us comfortable and still. I stroked her soft hair, and we gazed at the stars.

After a moment, I felt her lips on my neck. I closed my eyes and disappeared into the sensation. Soon, she was kissing my face, chin, cheeks, and eyelids. I opened them and looked at her, and, watching me back, she began to kiss my lips.

I kissed her back, eagerly, but slowly, too. I didn't want to get too excited, but I didn't want it to end, either. I stroked her back and shoulders, and she caressed my neck. Soon, the pace began to pick up a bit, though, inevitably, and I began to feel that stirring between my legs.

I pulled away, gently but firmly. "We have to stop."

Heidi groaned. "I don't want to stop." Her kisses

persisted, and my little southern pal began to pay more and more attention.

I had to push her away and sit up. "No, Heidi. I mean, we have to stop." I gestured loosely, and with embarrassment, toward my unit. "Just saying, you know?"

"Oh." She giggled and straightened her dress a bit. We were both breathing kind of hard, so we took a minute to pull ourselves together.

I felt her hand on my back. "I can't wait until we can just, you know, let it go."

Groaning, I turned to her and pulled her to me. "You're telling me," I whispered. "Guess we'll really have to pace ourselves on Saturday night. Maybe we should make some rules."

"Screw the rules," she said into my neck.

I held her like that for a long time. By the time we actually pulled apart we both knew it was time to go our separate ways for the night; it wouldn't do to push it. Both of us wanted something that we couldn't have right then, and like kids in a candy shop with no money, the best course of action was to leave before we started shoplifting.

At her door, we kissed again, but this time we kept it brief, which I learned was much easier to do if you're not lying pressed together.

"I'll see you in the morning?" she mumbled against my lips.

I moaned. "Yes, you will. Nine?"

"Mmm-hmmm."

Pulling away, I smiled at her. "See you then, gorgeous."

As I walked back to my stateroom, I felt weak, yet I also felt like I could take on the world. I didn't think I'd be able to leave her when the time came, and I started to entertain bad ideas in my head. I wanted to be with her all the time; to be apart seemed like death to me.

I pushed it all away and kept going. I would see her in the morning. The best thing to do right then was get to bed so the time would pass.

CHAPTER 19

Even though I tried, I couldn't seem to get those 'bad ideas' out of my head.

I lay in my bed that night, tossing and turning for the first two hours; sure, the nap hadn't helped the matter. But once I got the thoughts I was having in my head, it seemed I kept turning them over and over, at a breakneck pace, and I just couldn't settle. Finally, I gave in and just let myself dream.

What if, when we docked at Port of Miami, Heidi and I just 'took off'? What would we do for money? My father had taken my bank card. I could get a job. I had worked for a couple of summers for my Uncle Tank, he owned a construction company in Chicago, and he paid pretty well for guys to do clean up and assistance. I could put that down as experience, and I was a fast learner.

We could go to Vegas and get married. We didn't have to worry about ever seeing the ocean again if we didn't want to. We could get a little apartment, just like young, eloping couples do in the movies. We could carve out our own little piece of heaven, and no one could stop us.

By midnight I had done more than just daydream, I had formed what I considered to be a solid, foolproof plan of escape. All I had to do was convince Heidi that we should. I would have to do something to my parents I had never, ever considered doing before: I would have to steal from them. I would have to take my bank card back.

If we ran away, and my parents knew I had the card, they wouldn't stop usage or block it. I knew they would be too worried, and they would want me to have money. They would also want to track where I was using it, but I had that all figured out.

I would talk to Heidi in the morning, over our breakfast. I was sure she would see my point of view, and if not, I would do all I could to convince her. It wasn't until I had it settled in my head that I finally dozed off.

I slept like a baby.

∞

"So, have you ever been to Las Vegas?"

Heidi was working on a massive mouthful of French toast. Her cheeks were puffed out like a chipmunk, and I had to wait for her to swallow. My own food sat almost untouched before me. I had cut it up and pushed it around, but now my fork sat with it, all forgotten.

She swallowed and took a couple gulps of milk. "Vegas? Once; why?"

Time to pick up my fork and start pushing food around again. All of a sudden my little plan sounded a bit foolish to me, and I was almost scared to bring it up.

I tried to focus on how sure I had felt in bed last night. Finally, I just said to myself, screw it, and I started to spit it out slowly.

"Well, I spent a lot of time thinking last night," I began. "About us and all."

Heidi had stopped eating, and she gave me her full attention.

"Um…" Was I nervous! "Look, Heidi. I think when we get to the port and dock that you and I should… run away together."

There. I said it.

When I did finally say it, I did so while staring at the food I was pushing around. I waited, but when I realized it was taking her a mighty long time to respond I looked up at her. Believe me, I did so very slowly, bracing myself mentally for the worst.

She was just looking at me. There was no shocked, angry, or disgusted look on her face. Actually, she appeared to be thinking it through. I just waited and kept playing with my food.

"Well," she finally said, "It's a pretty tempting idea. But realistically, I don't think it will ever work."

"Why not?"

Heidi took a deep breath. "I have a cousin. She got married when she graduated high school. I mean, immediately. Her husband got a job working on cars, and they even had a cute little place to live. But they are divorced now; didn't make it a year. They were crazy in love."

She paused, and I didn't say a word; I knew she

wasn't finished.

"If there was anything I learned from that, it was that being a grown up and having a family is hard enough, even for those who wait and do it in time. But to jump the gun can mean death, you know?"

"I would have money from my college account," I said quickly. "I would get a job, and we would be more than comfortable. I would even attend community college at night, so I wouldn't be giving up. We could get married there, Heidi, so you wouldn't be going against your promise."

"It would break my father's heart to not walk me down the aisle," she said sadly. "He likes you now, very much. And if things work out, he is behind us fully. He told me. But if we do this, he would despise you; he would feel like you stole something from him he would never get back."

We fell into silence. She was right; I was thinking only of myself, not of how our parents would feel. There were more people to consider here than just Heidi and me.

"You're right," I said simply. I sat back in my booth and nodded my head. "While it might work, it would leave casualties."

She reached across the table for my hand, and I gave it to her. "We don't have to rush. This is going to work out; wait and see. I love you, and you love me, and miles mean nothing if it's real. If it's not, then the miles will prove it. That's how I see it."

I hated that she even thought this could be a simple

crush. "Miles will prove it?" I echoed. "So, even you have your doubts."

"Tripp, that's not what I mean, and you know it."

I shook my head; my emotions were getting the best of me, and my feelings were hurt.

"You think you might find someone better, fall in love with someone else," I spat, tears forming in my eyes. "Maybe you don't love me at all. For all I know, this is some kind of 'cruise ship fun' to you, right?"

Heidi looked hurt. "That's not true."

I stood up and threw my napkin down in the middle of my plate. "Well, maybe you should think about it for a minute. Why don't you come to find me if you change your mind?"

I skulked off. My pride was hurt, and I was a stupid kid.

The first thing I did was go back to the stateroom; I wanted to be alone. So what if I left her there? It wasn't like we were in the middle of a big city. We were on a ship in the middle of the sea, for Pete's sake. Besides, she had so much as said she wanted to see other people. Some 'relationship.'

My parents weren't there when I arrived, and I was relieved. I shut myself up in my room and lay on my bed fuming. I wouldn't leave the stateroom for the rest of the cruise; if she wanted me, she would have to come for me. Obviously, I had misjudged her feelings. I felt sick.

After ten minutes of acting like an idiot I began to get bored; after fifteen I started to question whether or not I was acting foolish, and after twenty I was positive I was the world's biggest moron.

Now I was pacing around my tiny room. She was right, of course. Time was the best, especially at our age. Didn't we both have goals and dreams? We needed to at least finish high school for that, duh. Of course, she loved me, and I knew it. Soon, I had to admit I had been mean, egotistic, and unfair.

Now I just had to work up my nerve and fix it. For all I knew, I blew it for good. But I at least owed it to her to apologize. I just had to go do it, and right then I couldn't bring myself to even leave my room.

I heard my parents come in; they were laughing and joking, though I couldn't really make out their words. Great, I was going to have to see them, and they would want to know why I was here. I'm a rotten liar; I would never be able to make something up. Besides, my mother would see it in my eyes right away that something was off; she was like a psychic or something.

But I didn't have to worry. After a few minutes I listened to the sound of them leaving, and I heard the stateroom door close. I sighed with relief and plopped down on my bed. I had to think of how to apologize to Heidi if she would even talk to me. How could I have been so rude to her? I left her sitting alone at the American Icon! The thought made me groan, and I lay back on my bed hard, my hand over my eyes.

I heard a light knocking on the door.

I sat up quickly and listened closely; I might have been hearing things. No, there it was again! Oh, no!

What if she had told her father what I had done, and he was here to chew me out?

I stood and left my room, dread filling my heart. Best to face it; I owed her an apology anyway. If it were her dad, I would take my chewing out like a man. A sixteen-year-old, trembling boy who had just left his daughter at the breakfast table with false accusations and real tears.

The knock came for a third time, just as I reached the door. It was louder and more insistent this time, so I picked up the pace. "I'm coming!"

I grabbed the knob and turned it, beginning to speak before it was even open. "Mr. Collins, I'm sorry."

But it wasn't Ted; it was Heidi. She was standing there with red-rimmed eyes and smudged eye makeup. She had a tissue wadded up in her hand, and her arms were crossed defensively over her chest.

"I have some things to say to you, Tripp Young, and you are going to let me in and listen." She pushed past me like my body was no more than a light, airy curtain fluttering in her way. She turned around, and I noticed her foot was tapping. "Sit down, please."

I was frozen in my spot. "Sit!" This time she almost yelled, so I sat. She was pissed.

Now she was pacing back and forth before me, and I felt like a kid who was about to get torn into by his mom or dad. After a minute, she spun in my direction and stopped. I braced myself right away.

"You have a lot of nerve, Tripp! Do you know that?"

I didn't know if that qualified as a question she wanted me to answer, or if I was supposed to just let it sink in so she could continue her speech. She kept staring at me, so I slowly nodded. Satisfied, she began pacing again, continuing as she did so.

"You know, I've never said 'I love you' to a boy in my life," she growled. "As a matter of fact, I have gone on a handful of dates, and none of the boys I dated did I ever go out with twice. I've focused on my education and my future. Until I met you, anyway. You were different, so I let myself go. I must have been the biggest idiot alive!"

I shook my head but kept my mouth shut.

"Oh, yeah! 'Sucker' written right on my forehead." She was ranting a little bit. "You said some really mean stuff, stuff that was out of line, outright lies! I mean, for all I know you could be a really smooth character, just trying to get me to 'do it' with you, saying all the right stuff, stopping us from going all the way when all along all you were doing was grooming me to be another notch on your belt. Are you? Well, are you?!"

Another head shake. "Heidi…"

"No!" Don't you talk!" Now she had stopped again, and she was glaring at me. "You could be, but would I say anything like that to you just to hurt you? Never! But you, you didn't hesitate to use my feelings as tools to hurt me. I expected more."

I didn't even try to answer. I was a jerk, a so-and-so, a savage. I knew it; she was right.

She was tapping her foot again. "Well?"

"Well, what?"

"Arrgh!" Heidi threw her hands in the air in frustration.

I was confused. "I'm sorry, Heidi. I really am. I don't know what else to say. I was trying to think of how I was going to apologize to you when you came. I love you, and I screwed up, okay? I screwed up. I said things I shouldn't have, and I left you at the Icon alone. My behavior was inexcusable, and I'm so sorry."

I sat back again, and my shoulders dropped. I was done, I had said what I needed to say. It was up to her to believe me and forgive me or not.

I kept my eyes on my hands, which were sitting in my lap. After a bit, I saw her sit out of the corner of my eye. She was thinking, I knew, and it was best to let her do so. Obviously, she was much calmer; I would let the waters recede patiently.

Her voice was soft when she finally spoke. "When you brought up Vegas and the plan you had made, I'll be honest: I got excited. I said to myself, 'That's the solution! We can do it!' But I knew in my heart how wrong it would be to do that to those who love me the most."

I looked up at her to see her gazing at me. "The thought of us walking away from each other on Sunday makes me want to throw up," I muttered softly.

Heidi rose and came to me, sitting on the floor by my feet. She wrapped her arms around my legs and rested her head on my knee. "I haven't had a night that I didn't cry myself to sleep since the first time you kissed me. I know how you feel, but there is a right way… and there is a wrong one. I don't want regrets, and I don't want you to have any, especially when it comes to us."

I sighed and quickly brushed a tear from both my eyes. "What is meant to be will be, I guess. But what if it's not, Heidi? What if it's not?"

She looked up at me with her big blue eyes full of tears. "Then there's nothing we can do about it except make the most of right now."

I slid down to the floor next to her, and for the next fifteen minutes we held each other and cried together. Heidi finally grabbed a tissue, blew her nose, and then plucked one out of the box for me. She took my hand and stood up.

"It's time to get busy right now."

CHAPTER 20

Believe me when I say to you that there is only so much a young pair can do aboard a cruise ship.

On a ship the size of the 'Diamond of the Sea,' it is a lot like a stacked floating town. There is so much to do that you may not get to do everything, even if you try, especially if it is filled to capacity. But I have to be honest: Heidi and I had done a number of things, and on this day, after making up from our spat, neither of us had any interest in taking any new activity in, nor revisiting any familiar ones.

The air seemed thick and heavy, even as we talked, held hands, or kissed. We felt the pending separation as if it were upon us already, and it saddened our hearts to the point of seeming depression. Believe it or not, we spent most of that day, until that evening, in silence, doing nothing but enjoying each other's company.

Now, you may say it was due to the fight we had, but I have to disagree. We felt comfortable together that day, and to be honest, after we made up the situation didn't cross my mind again. I had rid myself of any thoughts of absconding with my young love because I knew that it was a plan that would never be brought to fruition. Both of us were accepting what was to come, and that was what the sadness and melancholy were all about. Heidi had said, "It's time to get busy right now," and that was simply what we were doing.

But it hurt.

Had we been keeping an eye on the time we may not have been so surprised when it flew by. We sat in deck chairs on Deck 13, resting, having walked around every Deck we could more than once. Both of us had begun to feel the passing of the day.

Heidi looked over at me. "I didn't wear my watch. What time is it?"

I lifted my arm over my head lazily and replied, "A couple minutes of five."

She chuckled softly. "We haven't even eaten lunch, and it's dinner time already. Oh, well. I don't have a huge appetite anyway. How about you? Are you hungry?"

I actually had to think about it before I gave her an answer; that's how far food was from my mind. "Um, a little, I guess. That's weird; usually, I could eat at the drop of a hat all day long. Where do you want to go?"

"Well," she muttered thoughtfully, "My parents are eating at the place we ate with Blake, you know, that day. They'll be out for a couple of hours because they'll have drinks after in the Solarium. How about we order in and watch a DVD or something?"

"They won't get mad?" I asked.

Heidi shook her head and stood up. "Like I said. They trust me."

She took me by the hand and pulled me to my feet, and we headed back for her cabin.

Her mother always brought a full carry-on of DVDs, she informed me as she unzipped the bag. Opening it, she revealed two rows of ten movies. I was surprised.

"Why do you bring these?" I questioned as I began pulling them out, one by one.

Heidi groaned. "It's in case someone gets sick, or doesn't feel like leaving the stateroom... you know, for any reason; just in case. We have an old portable player, too. It hooks up to the television with cables." She unzipped a side pocket, pulled out the small, foldable DVD player, and cords. "It's old school, I know, but I think it will be a nice and peaceful way to spend the evening. I'm thankful my mom's crazy when she does things like this!"

We started laughing, and a hard rap at the door alerted us to our food. While Heidi answered the door, I continued to go through the movies. We had ended up ordering a pepperoni pizza and sodas, which came faster than I would have ever guessed. We hadn't even chosen a movie to watch yet. Most of them seemed to be chick flicks, but I soon discovered that the ones on the bottom were much manlier genres.

"Die Hard!" I exclaimed. "This is an oldie but goody! Have you seen it?"

She looked at me and rolled her eyes as she approached, pushing the small cart with the food and drinks. "Um, only a million times. When's the last time you saw it?"

I placed it on the stack and reached in for the next. "It's been a while; years, actually."

"Let's watch it then; it is good."

I could feel my eyes light up. "You don't mind?"

My girl just chuckled and shook her head. "Men."

So, that was what we did that last Friday night. We stayed in and ate pizza and watched 'Die Hard.' The two of us sat close on the sofa, snuggling (we didn't lie down!), and it felt like home.

It had just ended, and we were picking up our mess when Heidi's parents returned. We all greeted each other, and she let them know that we had eaten and watched the movie. Her dad seemed very impressed that I had wanted to watch it, and I almost got pulled into talking about it with him. Heidi interrupted, though, informing them we had planned to take a walk before turning in.

The night was beautiful, with a nice, gentle cool breeze, and a sky as clear as crystal. Of course, we took to Deck 16, which, as usual, was basically void of passengers. There was one older couple on the elevator with us during the ride up; when we got off, we discovered the four of us would be alone. The four of us went our separate ways almost as soon as the doors opened.

We didn't go to our usual spot, though. Instead, we simply began to walk very slowly. We talked about our future plans; I told her about what colleges I was considering applying to, and she discussed her extended family. Heidi told me about her cousins, especially a little girl named Abigail, who was just six months old. When she spoke of that baby her eyes lit up so brightly they nearly outshined the deck lights. It filled me with warmth to watch her and listen.

So, we walked, up and down both sides of the deck, in a long oval. The couple who had come up with us were down at the opposite end from where we began, and when we came around to their location, they were standing at the railing, looking up at the stars. The old man's arm was around the woman as if he were trying to keep her warm. She may have had a chill; both of them wore sweat suits and sneakers.

When we passed by them, they turned and smiled at us. Both of us smiled back and offered passing hellos, which were given back. We continued on the couple quickly out of our minds.

Our conversation continued. Now we talked a bit about my parents, and what I thought the future might hold for them, considering their plans to leave their company. Heidi hoped that the dinner we were all having together the following evening would have a positive impact, not only on their perspective of ecology and nature but also on their attitudes as to what they might do professionally. She thought that, with the educations they had, they could find something productive, beneficial, and satisfying, that would help the sick environment rather than break it down even more.

Soon, we were approaching the old couple again. This time, they had taken seats in deck chairs, right at the location, they had been standing minutes before. We neared them, obligatory smiles ready. But as we neared, the woman spoke up in a friendly tone.

"It's a beautiful night, isn't it?"

I glanced at Heidi. She was smiling, so I said, "It is, isn't it?"

The woman looked up at the sky; she was quite beautiful, for an older woman. Her hair was pure white and long; she had the sides pulled back and held with sparkly clips. In the light, I could see that she wore makeup, and she was obviously content and happy.

She looked back to us, still smiling. "Remember when the water was blue?"

I felt my happy looks fading. Remember? I wouldn't forget. To me, when the blue left, it was the beginning of the end, and I knew it to be a fact in my heart. Both of us gave her a sad nod.

She read our faces like books. "I take it the bright, pretty colors aren't so wonderful to you?"

Still, we did not answer; we simply shook our heads.

Three more deck chairs were sitting there, and the old woman reached over and patted the one next to her. "I'm Helen Goodwin; this is my husband, Raymond." She gestured to the adoring man next to her. "What are your names?"

Once more I glanced to Heidi; she was already making her way to the deck chairs, almost eagerly, I might add. She sat down in the one next to Helen Goodwin, so I took the next one. All of a sudden, sitting down felt really good, and I easily settled in.

"No, the colors are… almost ugly to me," Heidi finally replied. "Not almost. They are. Oh, and I'm Heidi; this is Tripp."

Helen sat back in her chair. "Then you truly see them for what they are, not for what you wish they were. And 'Tripp,' huh? Interesting name."

Her statement caught my attention. "You aren't here to 'see the sea'?"

"Oh, heavens no!" Helen Goodwin gave a laugh, and her husband joined her; he took hold of her hand and gave it a squeeze. His eyes were filled with love. "We took the cruise to visit the new places when we docked, and enjoy the night sky. We saved up for this our entire lives; we just didn't know that by the time we were able to come that we would be floating in vile poison."

We fell into silence.

Mrs. Goodwin sighed. "You know, we're 'old' to you, and I suppose we are. I remember, as technology improved, there were many things that, while having their negative traits, mostly had positive. Because of that, they became commonplace. Take cellular phones or the Internet. Soon, no one could imagine life without them. Am I right?"

Both Heidi and I offered soft yeses, and she continued.

"That's what this is about, my dears," she said, her smile gone and her voice serious. "We have gone and made an irreversible mess, and the world is dressing it up in costumes and masks, trying to convince themselves that it is now commonplace and should be 'embraced.' But, as I'm sure you know, it is killing us."

There were no words that I could respond with. Helen Goodwin had made a simple, yet profound, observation, and it was right on target. The planet was dying, one resource at a time, and at our hands, and we were turning it into an amusement park so we could feel better.

It seemed that Ray Goodwin had something to say. "So disgusted were we that we almost didn't come. We almost canceled and took it as a loss." His thumb stroked his wife's hand as he spoke. "Then we found out that Helen was sick, and we chose to come anyway. Not for the sea, but for the things above it, and the things all around it. We decided to come for us."

Helen placed her free hand over her husband's as it held her other one. "I think we had to do it. We had to see what was really happening. You know, the world, the media, and the powers that be? They present it as a great and beautiful thing, and they would like us to believe that they have all of the repercussions under control."

"I know," I replied softly. "My mother and father both worked for the company that developed the chemical that spilled." My voice was full of shame; I heard it loud and clear.

"Really?" Helen asked. "How do you feel about that?"

I had to think about the question for a bit. "Well, until this cruise I despised it, and in my own way, I guess I despised them for it. We come on this cruise every year, to see the hues, and to photograph the hues. But I knew the truth: it was all about money."

Both of the Goodwins nodded, and Heidi took my hand to support me. Once the words started coming out, it seemed as though I couldn't stop them. I'll be honest with you; it felt good.

"But then all the stuff happened. The little girl died first, and then we passed that dead island." I had to stop and take a breath; my eyes were stinging as they tried to fill with tears, and I looked away so no one would see them. I had to breathe, or they would hear it in my voice.

I was finally able to continue. "Then my friend Drake tried to escape, and he took that steward hostage, and we all know how that turned out. But that was what it seemed to take to get my parents to see reality finally; they are quitting their jobs when we get back home to Chicago."

My words were met with more silence. At last Mrs. Goodwin said in a motherly voice, "I'm sorry, Tripp, that you had to experience any of this."

Heidi spoke. "Tomorrow our parents are having dinner with us. My dad works with a team in Miami Beach that is trying to attack the water pollution. I think it will be good for them to learn about the things that their company didn't want to tell them. They want to change."

"So, you two just met on this trip, then?" Mr. Goodwin sat forward a bit in his chair and offered us a broad smile with his words.

"Yeah," I replied. My voice was obviously unenthused.

"Ah," Helen Goodwin said. "I see. I take it you plan to keep in touch? I mean, not that it's any of my business, but anyone can tell by the way you two youngsters look at each other that you probably should. Besides, you're both far too young for a shipboard romance."

Heidi's next words both relieved me and filled me with love, for she had never spoken them directly to me before, and I needed desperately to hear them. "Oh, yes! We travel quite a bit so I will call him two or three times a week. We'll both be eighteen soon, and then we'll be able to actually travel to see each other. We hope to be together for good someday."

Mr. Goodwin slowly stood, then helped his wife up. Both of them smiled at us, and Helen Goodwin even gave both of us light embraces. As they prepared to leave us, he wrapped his arm protectively over her shoulders, and she zipped up her sweat suit jacket all the way to block out the chill.

"Just remember, kids, no matter what the future holds because of... all this." She made a wide gesture with her arm toward the sea around us. "You must keep a positive attitude. You must continue to have hope." She went quiet, and I thought I could see tears forming in her eyes. "You both be safe, and enjoy your lives."

Then the Goodwins walked away. Heidi and I sat in silence, and we barely even took notice when the elevator swallowed them up and carried them away. I was in fairly deep thought; Mrs. Goodwin was right. You had to have hope; for all we knew, the world could literally end tomorrow.

My eyes began to get heavy, and just when I was ready to ask Heidi if she was tired she said, "Are you ready to go back? We have a really full day tomorrow; we both need rest, I think."

So, we left the deck for our staterooms, our moods a bit forlorn. Mrs. Goodwin's words had sunk in, and I knew that the world could change in an instant, and probably would. I found myself hoping, even as we walked. I hoped desperately for college, and to marry Heidi. I hoped to have children someday. But most of all, I just hoped to live.

I dropped Heidi off and went back to my stateroom, which was silent and still. I could hear my dad snoring from their room, and the affection I felt made me smile. The obnoxious sound that my mother had learned to live with somehow brought me a level of comfort, just as it always had. Someday I would hear that sound no more; yes, things could, and would, change in an instant.

I tucked myself in my bed and went right to sleep.

R.W.K. Clark

CHAPTER 21

Saturday

With waking came the realization that I had been crying, but I didn't need the pillow to know that my heart was so heavy I didn't want to get out of bed. I woke at seven-thirty, and I lay there until nearly eight-fifteen, just thinking about the fact that tomorrow morning I would be getting off the ship, and walking away from Heidi. The thought was unbearable.

At last, I made myself get up. I showered, dressed, and hurriedly packed for the following day. I left out clean underwear, and took my tuxedo, safely protected in a zipper cover, out of the closet to wear for the festival that evening. The stupid thing was a formal affair... ugh.

I also made sure that the clothes I would be wearing after the festival would be sufficient for our night in the Solarium. I would wear jeans and a sweatshirt, and I chose one of the ship's blankets off my bed to take as well. I would change into these clothes after the festival, and I wanted them to be warm enough.

I heard my parents talking, and I stuck my head out of my room just in time to see them leaving.

"Hey! Don't forget: we are having dinner with Heidi tonight at The Grande."

They both turned to me and smiled. "Oh, I thought they wanted to go to Chops' Grille. Oh, well, The Grande it is. Looking forward to it," my mother said. "Did you sleep okay, Tripp? I heard you in the night; it sounded like you were up. Did you have a bad dream?"

I shook my head. "No. Didn't dream at all."

"Hmm," she mused. "Anyway, we'll see you when we see you; love you."

"I love you too, Mom."

They left, and I got ready to do the same. I was picking up Heidi for breakfast in five minutes, and she was probably already waiting. I didn't want to stand her up for any reason during our last full day together.

We opted for a light breakfast. Knowing that we would still eat lunch, then have a massive and hearty meal with our parents before the festival, we thought it was important to keep our appetites. That's not even taking into consideration the fact that neither of us really had an appetite anyway.

Our choice for breakfast was the Windjammer Buffet. We decided as we walked that neither of us really wanted to spend too much time eating. The day was going by way faster than either one of us wanted it to, so the best thing we could do was waste as little of it as possible.

So, Heidi had yogurt with granola and a café latte while I ate an apple turnover with milk and coffee. We ate without talking; there were no concrete plans to make for the day's events; we were sort of going to go by the seats of our pants. The first step to get things rolling was to eat and get moving.

Surprisingly, we ended up wandering and just checking things out. We joked and laughed more than I would have thought possible, considering the circumstances, and it was a very enjoyable feeling. About mid-morning we found ourselves at Adventure Ocean, which is basically a place with activities for kids and teens; many of the passengers our age hung out there, though I had never been one to take advantage. That day, though, we did. We didn't hang out there to meet friends; that would be ridiculous on the last day of the cruise. But we just sort of disappeared in the midst of the young, carefree laughter and hollering going on around us. It turned out to be an effective way to be alone, without being alone at all.

Many of the kids were swimming in the pool, which was filled with AquaSim, of course. There weren't many there, maybe ten or fifteen other kids, but they all seemed to hang out in little groups of their own, cliques that had formed when they boarded. Heidi and I were a clique all our own, and we didn't need any other members.

We passed on the pool play, choosing instead to sit and watch the playing going on in it. A small kid's pool was about fifteen feet away from where we sat, and we watched as the kids, supervised by teen babysitters arranged by the Adventure Ocean program, splashed and frolicked without a care in the world.

In the large pool, the older kids were playing water volleyball. It was entertaining at times, and we managed to glean a few laughs out of it, but the small kids were much more satisfying. Something about their innocence made you forget about the state of the world, but at the same time, it made you want to just curl up and hide until you became a child again.

Which was never, of course.

Lunchtime was upon us in no time at all. We didn't have to speak to figure out where to eat. Without words, we took each other's hand and made our way back to Windjammer. The food was good, and the buffet-style dining made it easy to choose, sit, and eat without waiting for cooking or service. We both chose yummy-looking green salads with chicken in them, and we doctored them up to our liking.

We didn't have to go to our staterooms to dress for dinner until four. We would have dinner at five, and the Festival of Hues was to begin at six-thirty. I had attended the festival before; it started with a live brass band, and people mingled while members of the crew walked around with trays of hors d'oeuvres and beverages, both for adults and the younger set.

At that point, the captain would take the stage and spend a half-hour to forty-five minutes discussing the highlights (and, in this case, lowlights) of the cruise. I wondered what he would have to say; it was sure to be a much more somber and serious speech than those I had heard on previous cruises. After he was finished, when twilight had set in, the fireworks would begin.

There is an important point to keep in mind: the fireworks were not set off for the sake and beauty of the fireworks themselves. The whole point of the Festival of Hues was to draw attention to the disgusting water and its façade of colors. Passengers were supposed to look at the water when the fireworks went off because the light from the fireworks had a very strange effect when they reflected off it: they made the water look like liquid fire, frightening, yet boldly beautiful all at once. The water proved to captivate, and the fireworks mostly went forgotten.

While we ate, Heidi and I decided that we would determine to watch only the fireworks. We would sit back from the railing in deck chairs, and we would focus our eyes on the sky above us. It would be wonderful to enjoy the true beauty of this 'occasion,' and we would not let deceptive things keep us from it.

By twelve-thirty we were finished, neither of us had finished our entire salads. We had three-and-a-half hours; what we could do to fill it was a no-brainer. We would spend it in our favorite deck chairs on Deck 16.

You might have thought we would have tried to have more 'fun' together during this time. Maybe you were waiting for us to sneak off and jump in the sack so we could have furious, awkward teen sex before we were ripped apart, regardless of vows to dads or the responsibility it may entail. Maybe you just wanted to hear about everything being perfect during our last day together.

It was perfect, but not the kind of perfect you may

expect. Sure, we didn't indulge in activities or take advantage of a movie. We didn't spend the time making out like crazy or having sex; we didn't try to numb the pain with senseless superficialities. Rather, we chose to just be together and to feel the pain in all of its horrendous glory.

We kept it simple. We held hands, we talked a bit, and we cried. For most of the early afternoon, we held each other. It was lucky that no one bothered us or asked if we were okay. For some reason, we were granted the gift of being left utterly and completely alone, and that was how we wanted it. Heidi and I just wanted to process all that had happened, and what was due to take place, and we wanted to do it together.

"When we were talking to the Goodwins last night you said something," I told her at one point. "It was something I needed to hear, and I was so glad you said it. I hope you meant it."

We were lying in a single deck chair together, side by side, just holding each other and staring at the blue sky. It was very peaceful, and I think I can speak for both of us when I say that I was more comfortable and relaxed than I had been the entire trip. Yes, that was true, even though my heart was breaking.

"About calling you, you mean." It was a statement, not a question, and she didn't wait for a response. "Of course I meant it. Did you think you could give me your number and I really wouldn't call, Tripp?"

"I guess I'm just... afraid."

Heidi put her hand on my cheek and turned my face

toward hers. Then she looked deep into my eyes and said, "I promise, you will hear from me, and you will hear from me often."

We kissed, and I felt the weight of a thousand duffel bags lift off my shoulders. She would call me, and we would talk late into the night about anything and everything. Then, one day, our phone conversation would consist of flight plans and pick up times, and we would be together again.

Before I knew it, it was nearly four. We picked ourselves up and trudged our way to her stateroom, where it took us an additional ten minutes to part ways. I felt so sick all the way to my own cabin that I hardly remember the walk, and I have no idea how I found my way without getting lost. How could I keep going this evening knowing that the only girl I had ever cared about was going to be taken from me?

But I didn't have a choice. It would break her heart to watch me fall apart, and I had to maintain. I would shower again, power-slam some coffee in the room, which I would make as soon as I got there, and I would change my attitude for the better.

So, I set about the tasks before me, a whistle on my lips and tears in my eyes.

R.W.K. Clark

CHAPTER 22

"So, Jim, Heidi tells me you and Kate are going to be changing jobs when we get back to the mainland."

Ted Collins spoke with a pleasant voice to my father as he stabbed at a bite of his steak. I glanced at my dad when he asked the question; I hoped he wouldn't be offended at its somewhat personal nature. One look told me that my worries were unwarranted. The look on his face was eager and responsive.

"As a matter of fact, I am proud to say that we are," my dad replied. "You know, I believe both of us knew this was all wrong in our hearts, but we were a bit blinded, much to my regret." He looked up at Mr. Collins. "But I don't regret the decision to leave at all."

That simple question set off a marathon adult conversation of apocalyptic proportions. Heidi and I just held hands, sat back, and listened. It was good, I must say. Our parents got along very well, and mine were extremely receptive to all the little bits of information about the spill, and the chemical's effects, that Ted Collins offered up. They had been deceived by the company they worked for, and it had been going on a very long time. It was clear now, and the future looked bright for the two of us.

For the first time that day, Heidi and I actually ate our fill. We were both ravenous, and while the adults talked and played with their food, we got more and more comfortable, until finally, we dug in and wound up gorging ourselves. Heidi had chicken and pasta with Brussels sprouts, and I had a 'manly' steak, baked potato, and corn. She gave me bites of hers, and I can attest that all of it was done to perfection.

Dessert was a crazy chocolate thing that I can't pronounce. It was like a chocolate sculpture, large enough for all of us, and when they brought it to the table, the waiter poured molten chocolate over it, melting it away and revealing a cake on the inside covered in berries. It was insane.

Before we all knew it, it was nearly six-thirty. By the time we got to Deck 16 the band was playing, and people were milling around with drinks in their hands, talking and laughing. The ladies all looked perfect and beautiful, and the men all appeared to be James Bond. It was plastic and phony, and I was pleased to see that our parents were talking. At one point, the Roths tried to elbow in, but it wasn't long before they wandered away, bored and uninterested with the conversation they had interrupted.

So, with the adults busy with each other, Heidi and I were free to just roam around and watch people. We studied their faces and their body language, especially if they were at the railing, looking down at the rainbow-colored churning below. It turned out to be an interesting social experiment.

Now, due to the occurrences which had taken place earlier on during the cruise, the number of passengers onboard had dwindled significantly. Compared to years before, the Festival of Hues seemed sparsely populated, with a mere scattering of people here and there on all three of the decks being used for the festival: Deck 14, Deck 15, and Deck 16. We visited each and every one, in turn, just strolling around and watching.

Most people we saw looked down into the sick water and either laughed, pointed, or looked otherwise enthused and entertained. A couple of parents lifted their small child just high enough to see before quickly putting their feet firmly back on deck. I found that to be so hypocritical; they wanted to watch the sea in awe and wonder, and they wanted their kids to see it, but they didn't trust it even to touch it, much less with their child. It was both depressing and infuriating, to tell the truth.

But on the other side of the coin, there were those who, if they were looking over the railing, allowed their expressions to show the disgust they felt. There was a particular couple we passed who were busy telling their pre-teen son all about the chemical spill, what it had done to the water, and what all of it meant to the future of the planet. He was white as a ghost as if he had no idea, and I knew that he wasn't being filled in at school. Heidi and I talked a bit about that little family; their conversation made us angry that it had to be discussed and explained to kids at all, but we also felt invigorated that there were those out there who knew the truth.

We arrived back on Deck 16 just as the captain was beginning his long, redundant speech. I rolled my eyes at Heidi and feigned a yawn, and we both laughed and laughed before turning our attention to his words. I hoped that he would keep everything on a serious note; after all, this had been a long, painful, and unforgettable cruise.

He started with the usual baloney: thanks for joining us on the ship, we appreciate your patronage and always enjoy serving your cruise needs, blah, blah, blah. He then went into the tragedies which had taken place on board.

He talked about Sarah Mills but didn't mention her name. She would be commemorated in the upcoming Sarah Mills Children's Play Center, which would be on the 'Diamond of the Sea' cruise ships by the following year. He even paused to pretend to shed the obligatory tear.

The captain talked about the dead island next. He made sure to drive the point home that science and the government would be working together, hand in hand, to tend to the destruction being caused by the tainted water. Suddenly, the look on his face and the sound of his voice made me listen more closely; he didn't seem to be enjoying himself, not like years before.

Lastly, he discussed the deaths of Drake and the steward; it was at this point that the captain lost all ability to fake his emotions. At first, his voice became halted and scratchy, and then he simply broke down and cried. Everyone fell silent at that point.

When he had pulled himself together, he apologized. He told us all that if there was one single thing he had learned from this cruise it was how wrong he had been about the water. He apologized yet again, this time for leading the way out into the middle of it by captaining a cruise ship in those troubled times. He announced that he would be retiring after we docked, and he made it a point to thank all those he had served year after year for his career.

As his final coup de grace, the captain of 'Diamond of the Sea' began to give a lecture. He talked about the sea, and how productive it used to be, beautiful and teeming with life. We trusted it to swim in and fish in; we didn't fear getting wet. It sustained life the world over: the animals, plants, people, and the planet as a whole. He said he didn't want to talk about the truth of what the future held, but he was sure we all knew in our hearts. We were implored to face that truth and stop glorifying it. We were implored to all change our ways, just as he was, and save ourselves.

With that, he wrapped up his speech. The crowd stood silent and stunned, us included, before him. I couldn't say what the other passengers on other decks, who were listening over a television, looked like, but I was sure their faces were the same.

"So, tonight is the Festival of Hues," he said at last, arms raised in the air. His voice was more cheered, but his eyes were mourning. "This festival is a 'Diamond of the Sea' tradition dating back to the spill. Some of you will love the effect of the fireworks on the water, but tonight, I encourage you to pay attention to the skies. Look up and forward; let's treat this poisonous, murderous water as the true pariah that it should be!"

Right then, the first fireworks went off. Heidi and I found two deck chairs, and we sat down, reclining comfortably, without a care. They burst in the night, lighting up the sky as though the sun were returning for an encore. I watched intently, tears in my eyes, holding the hand of my beautiful love, and wishing all of this were taking place under different circumstances.

At one point, I looked at the railing. There were far fewer people leaning over to see the water than I expected, and I saw no cameras flashing, at least, not right there. What I did see, surprisingly enough, were people who were finally getting it, and in the light of the explosions, I saw many, many tears fall that night.

We didn't stay to watch the grand finale. Instead, both of us headed to our staterooms to change, and we met up at the Solarium, jackets on and folded blankets in hand. We met each other with smiles, and without a word, headed to see if the deck chairs we had chosen were free.

CHAPTER 23

The first thing I did after we found our deck chairs (yes, the ones we wanted!) was to find a deckhand or steward. I wanted to ensure there would be no trouble at all, at any time during the night, while we were there. Honesty was the best policy, my parents taught me, so I went to let someone know of our intentions.

Fortunately, just as we had predicted, the decks were clearing out. People were heading to their cabins and staterooms to prepare for docking the following morning, and the few stragglers who remained were mostly at the bar. I found a deckhand there, visiting with a passenger who appeared to be nursing a glass of straight whiskey.

"Excuse me, sir," I interrupted gently. "I was wondering if I could have a word with you for a moment?"

At first, the young man looked confused, but he soon followed me to a private spot about ten feet away.

"How can I help you?" he asked.

I proceeded to explain what Heidi and I were planning to do. I did so carefully, making sure he understood that we weren't delinquents, nor did we intend to have sex there. I made sure he understood the circumstances: we were in love, and the next day we would be separated. He could contact our parents if he desired; we had their permission and would confirm it for anyone who asked.

When I was finished, the man, who was only about twenty-two or so himself, looked around the deck conspiratorially. He turned back to me and offered me a wink. I didn't know whether to laugh or just stand there looking stupid.

"Where do you plan to be?"

I pointed to our chairs, two in a row of four, with Heidi in the first one, her back to us. He nodded, looking a bit relieved. His reaction was good so far.

"I'll tell you what," he said, "this is the least busy night of the cruise. I don't think there will be a problem. I'm on until three in the morning; then I will let my relief know you are there. But we need to have you up and out of here by seven-thirty at the latest. Do you need someone to wake you?"

I told him no, and set the alarm on my watch right in front of him. "Thank you so much," I said. "It sounds corny, but this means a lot to both of us."

He shook his head. "Not at all. With all that's going on in the world, love is all any of us really have in the end."

With that, he gave me a firm clap on the shoulder and walked away.

I went back to Heidi and began to make myself comfortable. She was already settled in; she had pushed the chairs together and put two bottles of orange juice next to each so we could reach them. Soon, we looked like a couple of peas on a pod, reclined and covered up, holding hands and staring at the night sky.

I must have dozed off because the next thing I knew Heidi was saying, "Hi! I'm glad to see you again before we dock!"

My eyes flew open to see Mr. and Mrs. Goodwin. "Good morning, sleepyhead!" Mr. Goodwin joked.

I glanced at my watch; it was ten-thirty. The Solarium was very quiet and peaceful, and a quick glance over my shoulder told me it was almost void of visitors. I sat up and ran my hand through my hair.

"Hi. What are you two doing out so late?" I asked.

Helen smiled at us both. "Do you mind if we sit for just a bit? We won't stay long; it's long past our bedtime. We just wanted to take one more jaunt, you know, to enjoy the solitude for once."

We both nodded, and the pair sat in the two empty chairs next to me. For a couple of minutes, no one spoke. At last, Ray Goodwin broke the silence.

"What did you two think of the captain's speech?"

It was a good question, and one I was waiting for someone to ask. Heidi, who had gotten to know me so well, let me speak first. I was anxious to discuss it, no matter how briefly.

"I think he was on point all the way," I began, "and I'm glad he has made a decision, from the heart, to walk away from this."

Helen agreed with a slight hum. "What did you think

about what he insinuated about… the future? About what this would eventually do?"

I knew right away what she was asking. I looked at Heidi to see her sad eyes watching me, trying to see how I would react and what I would say. I thought about it; I didn't want to just shoot out meaningless baloney. I wanted to tell the truth.

"I know in my heart he's right." I cleared my throat to get rid of the frog that was in it. "This isn't going to end well at all. Best we don't feed the monster."

"This is a fact." Helen Goodwin didn't hesitate. "The plants will all die and take the oxygen with them. Important insects are being wiped out, and animals all over are dropping dead; people too, here and there. It's a matter of time, kids. Know that, and don't waste any of what you have left." She sat up from her position in the deck chair and turned her full attention on both of us. "Just know that facts are facts; don't live in denial. Live your life to the fullest, as we are. Don't have unrealistic expectations about this being miraculously fixed. I'm not trying to be harsh; I'm just being honest."

The old pair stood up, and Ray automatically put a protective arm around his wife. "I hope all goes well for the both of you. We'll be thinking of you. Have a good night."

They walked off into the night, leaving us there in almost stunned silence. Both of us just sat there for the longest time, staring at the sky and thinking. I didn't feel any fear or dread, just a surety about the truth that I was learning to accept.

"I wonder what it will be like," Heidi finally muttered.

I turned to her. "What?"

"The end."

I thought about that. I thought about the little girl in the crawlspace and the black, dead island surrounded by the corpses of wildlife and the dead sea. I thought about Drake and the steward, and the second they fell into the water.

"It will be fast. However it comes, Heidi. It will be so fast."

She rose off of her chair and joined me on mine. We folded her blanket and made a pillow out of it, then I held her, my arm around her tightly and her head on my shoulder. Soon, her breathing evened out, and I knew she was sleeping.

Then, and only then, did I let the tears fall. I cried for the world, and I cried for all in it. I cried in silence for the dead, and for all who would die. I cried for the way things used to be, and would never be again.

But most of all, I cried for Heidi and me, and what I hoped would be someday.

I couldn't tell you how long I lay there, wide awake, holding the most beautiful girl in the world, but it was for hours. Not once did I bother to look at the clock, because time didn't matter. All that mattered was that very second, all of them, and I wouldn't let them pass so easily.

At last I slept, and I dreamed of a girl with long red hair, wearing a white dress, and running to meet me as I got off an airplane…

CHAPTER 24

Sunday

The day that, even now, proved to be one of the worst of my life.

It started with me waking at four-thirty in the morning. My arm was dead asleep, and there was Heidi, nestled snuggly and sleeping soundly on it, just as she had fallen asleep. I carefully and gently worked it out from under her, then stood to shake it out and walk it off.

After a bit, I wandered off, making sure no one was around to bother Heidi and found the men's room. I had to go badly, and I hadn't even touched my orange juice. I figured it was all the soda and sparkling grape juice from the night before, and as I let it go, I breathed out the immense relief that came with it.

When I returned, Heidi was still sleeping soundly, but she had turned over and pulled the blanket over her head. Rather than wake her, or even disturb her slightly, I sat in one of the other chairs, and I just watched her sleep. The only things peeking out were her red hair and her forehead; I thought it was the best and most beautiful forehead I had ever seen.

Believe it or not, I did this for some time: two hours, to be exact. At six-thirty I went to the bar and asked for two coffees, which the bartender served up immediately. I made my way back to her slowly, eager to wake her.

"Heidi," I said softly, "rise and shine."

The blanket came down slowly, and as soon as her eyes met mine, we broke out into smiles. But they lasted only a second. Soon, hers faded, and she looked at me sadly.

"It's Sunday."

I nodded and held back my tears. "Yes, it is. I brought you coffee."

Heidi sat up and gingerly took the cup from me. For about ten minutes we sipped the steamy brew, letting it melt the cobwebs of sleep from our brains. Then, she put her cup on the deck and looked at me.

"We have to be strong," she said. "We have to be mature, and we have to be strong. We must remember that we will talk, and see each other, too. We have a future."

"I know."

Heidi dropped to her knees before me abruptly, put her arms around my midsection, and rested her head on my lap. I put my coffee down as well and began to stroke her hair. She needed a minute, and so did I. With the rising of the sun came the reality, hard and cold.

"Distance won't keep us apart," I whispered. "We'll be eighteen before you know it, and we'll talk all the time, as often as you want."

She nodded but didn't speak. She just kept her head

down, and I knew she was savoring the moment. I stopped trying to fix her feelings and joined her. After all, it was the last real chance we had to be alone.

Seven-thirty came all too quickly. Crew members began to rush around in preparation for docking, and we would be nothing but in the way soon. I brushed Heidi's hair away from her face and took her chin, tilting her head up toward me.

"We have to go," I said. "Our parents are waiting, and we'll dock by nine."

With a deep breath, she rose, and I followed. We gathered the few things we had with us in silence, then took each other by the hand and headed back to Heidi's staterooms very slowly. Too soon, we were at her door.

She turned to me quickly. "I love you. I will always love you."

"I love you, too," I assured her sincerely, with much emotion. "We will have time to say goodbye on shore; our parents will let us. You have my number, right? Good. We can all get off together, and then we can take time to do this."

But she didn't listen. She dropped her blanket to the floor and flung herself into my arms. I held her tightly and kissed the top of her head over and over. I had to be strong, just as she had been with me when I talked about running away. I had to support her, and us, to do the right thing, and I had to make it as easy as possible.

I knew, right then, that the easiest thing, the best thing for both of us, was to let it hurt. She needed to cry, and so did I. We both needed reassurance, so we stood there, cried, and comforted each other.

But we had to keep going. With much convincing, I got her to go inside and help her parents get things wrapped up. I headed for my stateroom, looking over my shoulder over and over in case she came back out to me.

But, of course, she didn't.

∞

At nine-fifteen both my family and Heidi's family were in line to get off the 'Diamond of the Sea.'

Even though the process was chaotic, it was much smoother than in years gone by. Without all the passengers who had left in Mexico, things went much more smoothly than even I would have liked. It was all ending way too soon.

The baggage service had taken our things and would deliver them to the airport. We would head there directly to catch our flight home, while Heidi and her parents went to the port lot to pick up their car. According to Mr. Collins; they would drive home, spend the night there, and then fly to Mexico, where he would consult about the black island. They would barely get a break before facing the mess again, and I felt sorry for her.

By ten o'clock the four of us were standing just outside the main building at the port. I was shaking like a leaf, and I looked to my father. He nodded toward Heidi, and I went to her.

As soon as I reached her, her parents disappeared, going to talk to my own mom and dad so we could have a moment alone to say goodbye.

"So, I'll be talking to you soon?" I asked right away.

"As soon as we get to Mexico," she replied sadly. "I promise you. Within two days."

I nodded, and with tear-filled eyes, we embraced once more. Heidi turned her head up to me, and we kissed, passionately, but respectfully. All I felt was her love, and it shook me to my core. I hoped she felt mine, too.

"Oh, I don't want to let you go," I whispered.

She was sobbing, and nearly choked on her words. "Me neither, but we have to."

She pulled away and stood on her toes for one more kiss. Her parents appeared once again, so she stopped and said, "Be strong."

"Be strong, Heidi."

Ariana Collins put her hand on her daughter's shoulder; a shuttle was waiting to take them and their luggage to the lot. It was time. I could hardly bear it.

"You'll call me. You promised!" I cried out.

"I promise. I love you!" She said.

They were walking away now, and I kept my eyes glued to her for as long as I could. I watched as the shuttle pulled away with Heidi, sobbing, pressed against the window. The tears fell from my eyes uncontrollably now, and I began to follow the slow-moving vehicle.

But soon, I couldn't keep up anymore, and Heidi Collins was quickly gone from my sight.

My father had me in his arms then, and he let me sob. He didn't say a word, only held me. I think that was one of the single most loving things my father ever did for me in my life.

Just like that, she was gone.

CHAPTER 25

That had all taken place the summer of 2023, four years after the spill. It was the best two weeks of my life.

Yesterday I finished reading over all I had written up until now. It shook me up pretty badly, reading it all at once like that. It was as if I were reliving it all in one big bite, and I am glad I wrote it in bits and chunks over the course of time.

I cried myself to sleep last night and dreamed dreams that had no right coming to me. I thought, for the millionth time, about Heidi Collins; I could still remember the way she smelled, and the twinkle in her eye. I could clearly see the freckles on her nose.

Heidi never did call. Finding her in Mexico was impossible. For years, I let it hurt me. I took it personally, and tried to imagine who she ended up falling in love with that would make her forget me. You know, I never did marry, and I always held out hope that I would someday get that call. Until last year I jumped every time the phone rang, or I got a private message online, but it was never her.

Then, last year, I threw all caution to the wind. I had never tried to visit her; I thought it might damage the life she had built. But last year, I was sitting in my little windowless box home, breathing the pumped-in recycled air the government provided, and I decided that I, after nearly thirty years, deserved closure.

So, I set about finding her.

It took me two months. The Internet isn't the same as it used to be since they built the domes over us. Nothing is as it used to be. We travel through underground shuttle tubes from place to place, and all of us have to stay under the dome of our own country. We are prisoners of our own ingenuity, drinking fake water and breathing man-made air.

But I decided to look, and I did. That was when, after all the years I spent crying, wondering, and hurting, I learned that Heidi didn't blow me off for another man. She didn't simply forget me, as I had assumed.

Two days after we docked all those years ago, Miami Beach was hit with a hurricane. It wiped out the entire city. The water immediately killed every single living thing it came into contact with.

I had always assumed Heidi was safe in Mexico during that storm. But during my research, I stumbled on the truth: her name on a list among the dead. I don't know why she was still in Florida when the hurricane came, but she was. She was among the dead, a memory, and a dream that would never come to life.

I grieved all over again when I found out. I begged forgiveness for the bitterness, anger, and blame I had carried, directed all at my first, and only, love. It literally took me weeks to pull myself out of it.

That was when I decided to write this book.

I don't know what the state of this sick, forsaken planet will be in twenty years, or even five, for that matter. All I know is that I hope, if this is ever read by anyone, it clearly shows them what humans are capable of when driven by greed and deception. Those two, when combined, are nothing short of murder, whether anyone dies or not.

In this case, countless have, and still are. Cancer is taking us like flies. The sick die of dehydration and lack of proper oxygen. Babies are stillborn all the time. This plastic-coated world is a terrible place to live, and many of us just wish for it all to end.

As for me, I still love Heidi Collins, and I suppose I will until they shoot my corpse into space. I hope when I go, wherever I end up, she is there waiting for me, wearing that yellow and orange dress, and smiling with her arms wide open. I hope someday we can be together, and our time on that boat will amount to more than a heartbreaking memory.

So, I'll end this now, and offer it up to anyone who cares. Learn its lessons and feel its pain. Understand that both love and life are fleeting, and tomorrow is never promised to anyone.

I love you, Heidi Collins, and I always will.

ENTREATY

This book was made possible by reviews from readers like you. Reviews fuel my creativity. If you enjoyed this novel, I implore you to please write a review and share your experience on the retailer's website. The livelihood for authors is entirely dependent on reviews, and I must say, it is the largest obstacle as a struggling author that I have encountered. Please tell a friend, tell a loved one about this read. With your help, I will be one step closer to overcoming this obstacle. In return, I thank you from the bottom of my heart, and sincerely appreciate your time and effort.

Humbled, with gratitude,

R.W.K. Clark

ABOUT THE AUTHOR

I am a father of two beautiful children, Jon and Kim. They are my motivating forces; they are the lighthouse in this vast ocean. In my life, they are the air that I breathe; they are the oasis in this desert of uncertainty. They are my greatest joy in life and my number one priority. I have a long list of hobbies, and I attribute that to my lust for life! I like to surround myself with positive people, who share the same interests. Family values, the arts, outdoors, nature, and travel are tops on my list. I embrace attending cultural and artistic events because I believe dramatic self-expression is the window to the soul. I wear my heart on my sleeve, and I still believe in chivalry, and I always treat people the way I want to be treated.

www.rwkclark.com